FIRE ON WATER

Anthology #1

The Northshore Writers Group

Auckland, New Zealand

BRUCE WYNESS   ELIZABETH VILJOEN
A.J.S. IMMS   W.A. HAMILTON
SYLVIA APOSTOL   S. JAYNE BRADLEY
SHARRON MARTIN   SARAH ANDERSON
ADA MARIA SOTO   TIM OWEN
CHRISTOPHER MCKINSTRY

NORTHSHORESWRITERS.CO.NZ

Cover Art by ArtisticCustard

Published by Northshore Press

This edition published 2025

Contents

Introduction

The North Shore Writers' Group of Auckland, New Zealand, was founded in 2016 by Tim Owen. Upon arriving in New Zealand, Owen created the group to meet people with a common interest in creative writing. Before immigrating, Owen published three novels in the gay romance, psychological thriller, and young adult genres. He is currently working on a quirky Sci-fi.

Since the foundation in 2016, the group has had four major successes: Graci Kim went on to be a *New York Times* best seller, multiple award-winning writer Nikky Lee signed a three-book deal, Sharron Martin's *Discovering Orla* was published in September, and Frances Denny has just signed with literary agent Kate Davids of Arc Literary Management.

Denny's not yet officially released novel *My boyfriend Beelzebub* has already been shortlisted for the Page Turners Awards. They plan to go "on sub" (pitch to publishers) in November. Frances Denny first joined the group in 2017. She says she attended only one meeting and was extremely shy. Didn't attend another meeting until 2019. "What the group did," she now says, "was build my confidence to share my work, and created a supportive environment to receive, give feedback and root for each other.

Also, I want to thank the group for their support through a particularly traumatising event in my writing life. The group was there when I was feeling vulnerable. And their validation and encouragement through that time kept me writing." Her writing falls in the upper-young adult/new adult paranormal romance genre.

Speculative fiction author Nikky Lee says joining the North Shore Writers' Group gave her the accountability she needed to finish the book she'd been working on for 16 years, as well as writing and publishing over 20 short stories. "They have been there through the lows of the query trenches to the highs of award wins, and I absolutely would not be where I am today without them," says Lee whose novelette *Dingo & Sister* won the Best Young Adult Short Story and the Best Fantasy Novella categories in 2020. In 2021, she received a Ditmar Award for Best New Talent. Nikky's debut novel *The Rarkyn's Familiar* won the 2023 Sir Julius Vogel Award for Best Youth Novel, three 2022 Indie Ink Awards, Bronze in Young Adult Fiction at the 2022 Foreward Indies Book of the Year Awards and was a finalist in the 2022 Aurealis Awards for Best Young Adult Novel.

"The group is a sacred place of support, learning and joy for me. An opportunity to meet new people, share our writing, receive constructive, helpful feedback and find allies in the pursuit of the holy grail of publication. I am so grateful to be a part of it," says Irish author Sharron Martin whose debut romantic comedy was released in September.

The other members of the group are in various phases of working on their writing – some are in the final editing phase, others are submitting work to publishers, and many are producing new work weekly. The members write in a variety of genres, depending on the interest of the writers. The common factor is the dedication to producing works of excellence.

"It's awesome having people from different backgrounds sharing their writing in different genres that you would never be exposed to. From children's books to romance to chick lit to horror. Writing is damn hard and the support the group gives helps so much. It seems like every session I learn something new," says horror writer Andrew Imms.

Short story writer Bruce Wyness says, "It's not easy revealing your secret thoughts, speaking out loud the stories in your head and sharing those words, but with this group it has always felt safe. Their comments and suggestions reveal to me new ways to craft what I present. Their critique is always given with care and positive support. It's a lovely place to be."

For Su Bradley, the group offers support, accountability, friendship and constructive criticism. Since joining the group, she feels she has grown as a writer. She loves the group meetings at the Heart of Bays (the community centre) and at Pickles Café for writing sprints. "Also, I find the best movie, series and podcast recommendations here as well. I must point out the level of trust built between members, that no idea shared will ever be stolen. One of the best decisions I ever made, was joining this group."

"The group provides an encouraging and positive environment to practice and hone skills in. The atmosphere is informal but committed and it is so good to be with others who are just as passionate as you," says Young Adult fantasy writer Christopher McKinstry.

Science fiction writer Alex Hamilton recently moved back to Canada. He says, "When I joined the North Shore Writers' Group, I was just starting to work on my first novel. The feedback I received through the group helped me to build confidence in my writing, examine my story in new ways, and commit to finishing the project. I always looked forward to those Saturday morning meetings. It is a great community where you'll receive the advice and support you need to grow as a writer."

Joining this group has been amazing for Nicola Dickinson. Even though no one else is writing in her genre (picture books), she feels she gets such positive and helpful feedback. Thanks to the group, she has also found out about different competitions, workshops, helpful websites, and so much more. Plus, there's always the added incentive of getting some writing done, so she always has something new to read at our next meet-up!

When Elizabeth Viljoen immigrated from Namibia to New Zealand, she looked for an earnest writers' group who could support her with the novel she was writing. Not only was the North Shore Writers' Group walking distance from her new home, but their feedback gave her all the confidence and support she needed. At that stage she wasn't even sure which genre she was writing in, and she was tempted by all of their genres. The group encourages each writer to have their own voice, and soon she discovered that she was writing a family saga. That's the biggest strength of this group, in her opinion – that there is no peer pressure, only heartwarming encouragement.

Founder Tim Owen says that he loves how this writing group has brought such amazing people together. This first anthology of the North Shore Writers' Group is a work of love, something we have envisioned for a number of years to showcase the talent in the group. We've burned ships in this anthology, and the midnight oil. While building strong bridges. Over coffee at the Heart of Bays. And breakfast at Pickles.

Wait, not really – we've built plots and characters and weird fantasy worlds. And maybe this anthology is more a work of hate and revenge, if you read some of the short stories...

Valhalla

A woman visits her grandparents and surprises her grandfather in his workshop completing a secret project. She is dismayed once she discovers what it is and why he is making it.

About the author: Bruce Wyness
Bruce grew up in a small country town close to beaches, rivers, and farmland. Experiences from this time are reflected in his writing, mainly short fiction but also reimagining and retelling family history. He is an avid reader and an observer of people and uses that to craft his stories.

November 11, 2025. It is with a heavy heart that we say goodbye to Bruce as he finally succumbed to the cancer with which he was diagnosed a few years ago.
Forever in our hearts, Bruce.

"Hey Grandma, what a beautiful spring morning. I found some wild mushrooms along the old bridle path, and I picked some for you."

Grandma looked up from the quilt she was working on and peered into my bag.

"Oh poppet, they are just perfect, thank you! Put them on the bench, I'll make a steak and mushroom pie for you to take back home." She paused, then held up the quilt. "I've almost finished this quilt for you, see? It has many family memory squares on it."

Grandma was always baking and sewing and giving things away to her friends, neighbours and family. She had always been part of my life, and more so since the accident.

I propelled my wheelchair past the table to face her. She smiled, took my hands in hers and gently squeezed. I looked around the big open area; kitchen, dining and lounge in one space, with plenty of space for me to manoeuvre. I loved it here.

"Where's Grandad?" I asked.

She sighed and pulled a face. "Probably out in the garden or his shed. He's working on a secret project. Goodness knows what it is, but he's spent the last few days in there, only coming out when I call him for lunch and dinner. He was supposed to take his best friend Alfred out sailing on the yacht today but said he didn't have enough time for that and went out to his workshop."

"Well, I want to talk to him about making some toys for my students. I'll go and find him," I said, spinning around and down the ramp Grandad had built for me, then along the garden path.

"Farfar, Farfar, where are you?" I called and scanned the garden. It was overflowing with vegetables, some ready for harvesting, but he wasn't there. I turned the wheelchair past the tomato vines and towards his workshop.

Now I was closer I could hear one of the machines running, the big stroke sander, I think. He would have his earmuffs on and wouldn't hear me call. I pushed open the door but couldn't go in as there was a step up to the floor. There was a pile of oddly shaped timber on his workbench and lengths of smooth trim and scotia in a rack by the spindle moulder.

Grandad was concentrating on sanding the face of a board on his long sander. It looked like a piece of white satin birch, a favourite timber from his native Norway. I knew he had some slabs of it in the wood store behind the workshop. This must be a special piece of furniture, I thought. He had told me many times he was keeping it for something unique. 'A statement piece' he would say. As usual, wood shavings covered the floor, various hand tools were scattered on the workbench. A dust extractor was turned on sucking dust from the big sander. There was lots of noise and I knew he couldn't see or hear me. I took the underarm crutches out of the holder on the side of my wheelchair, hoisted myself up, moved into the workshop and sat on the small bench to wait until he'd finished.

Always interested in pieces he made, I looked at the timber on the bench and noted the beautiful finish, the perfect joins with concealed fixing, it was all book-matched too. This was indeed going to be a beautiful piece. It was a strange shape though, maybe some sort of offset coffee table or a bespoke dining table for an awkward space.

I didn't hear the sander stop.

"No! Get out, you can't be in here," Grandad yelled. "Please go now." He had never yelled at me. He always spoke quietly, with a Norwegian accent where w's became v's and o's were rounded like someone laughing when they talked. His words scared me. Why was he angry? I burst into tears.

Grandad came to me, squatted, and held me in his arms. "I'm sorry my love, but you can't see this." I hugged him and looked over his shoulder as he held me. It was then I realised what he was making.

"Farfar, why are you building a coffin?"

I leaned back to see him. He was tired, his strong face had sagged into a gathering of wrinkles. His eyes, once a striking blue, were dull.

"Oh, my precious barnebarn," he murmured, then pulled me close and held me tight. He began to sing. Softly at first but repeating the verse each time a little louder with each telling.

> Once alone a cry arose
> Half of anguish, half of pride
> As he sprang upon his feet
> With flames on every side
> "I am coming," said the King.

Grandad often sang Norwegian songs to me and told stories of his journey from his homeland. But this one I'd never heard before. I felt a strangeness as he sang. The words to me seemed both warlike and peaceful. It had a deep meaning for him as he sang it a few more times in the Nordic language. We held each other in silence for a long time and then he pulled away from me and stared into my eyes. He nodded and, seeming to have made a decision, he rose and brought my wheelchair into the workshop and helped me into it.

"Ah barnebarn, I am unwell," he said. "Bestomer does not know this, so I ask you not to tell her. It is my desire to go to Valhalla in the traditional way, and this is my Kista, my coffin."

A jumble of thoughts with no foundation collided in my mind, a tangle of words I couldn't speak, emotions I couldn't feel, my body numb. I reached out and took his gnarly hands in mine, felt the callouses, saw the scars, the mottled skin. I searched his face and in his eyes was the pain of past sadness, his skin was pale and stretched too thin.

"Oh Farfar, no, don't do this, please."

He walked to the door, locked it then turned off the lights. We sat in the gloom of his workshop and talked for a long time. He told me he had only a few weeks to live and was going out on his terms. I didn't try to change his mind; he was so sure of what he wanted and was content with the life he'd lived. His only regret he said would be leaving Grandma and me.

From outside the door, a shout, "Lunch is ready. Why are you two in there in the dark?" It was Grandma, of course.

"Sorry my dear, just looking at the grain on a burl, and it's easier without bright light. We're coming now," Grandad replied. He looked at me and put his finger to his lips. "Just you and me for now?"

I nodded slowly. Not sure how I could face Grandma knowing this secret; I loved them both so much.

Farfar and Bestomer had always worked in harmony in whatever they did. Each seemed to

11

anticipate what the other wanted or was thinking – a loving partnership. They had been married for 60 years and still used the little intimate signals and gestures that most couples had left behind. We chatted over the salami, cheese, pickle and bread that Grandma had prepared. She didn't ask about the project or what we had been talking about.

Grandad finished his lunch and stood. "I'm back in the workshop this afternoon. Will you be staying for dinner, barnebarn?" he asked.

"I'm not sure, but I'll stay and chat with Grandma for a while," I replied.

Grandma and I chatted for a few minutes while we cleared and stacked the plates to be washed. She sat down at the table and smiled at me. "Look at me, my love." She held my hands; her eyes were wide and clear. "He told you, didn't he?"

I thought of feigning ignorance but realised that was pointless. She knew. "Yes Bestemor, he told me. How did you know?"

She looked into my eyes, the edges of hers softened, the sunlight reflected in them.

"Of course, I know, we've been married for 60 years and been together for nearer 70. We have always supported each other's dreams and have been united in everything we've done," she paused for a moment, then added. "And we always will." She paused again, chuckled and said, "Besides he left the medical report on his desk, and I read it. I know he wants to have a Viking funeral, to live in Valhalla. I will allow him that as a gift when the time comes".

Grandma talked about the ceremony. "Grandad will be laid in his coffin, then his friends will propose countless toasts with aquavit. A feast fit for a king will be served, and many speeches will be made. Later he will be carried to his longship yacht. A sword and shield will be placed on the coffin, then the mainsail raised and the boat pushed out to sea. When it is well offshore, an archer will shoot a burning arrow into the air to land on the boat. The inferno will burn the ship and cremate his body."

Grandad's friends gathered at his home to farewell him. It was a day of high emotion, many tears and much laughter as stories were retold and memories recounted. The lawn out the back had trestles with plenty of food, much of it the Norwegian dishes he and Grandma loved. There was no formal service, just a gathering of people acknowledging the passing of their friend.

As the afternoon went on people shared anecdotes with the crowd. A lectern stood on a small, raised plinth and as the aquavit consumption rose so did the number of people who stepped up to it and spoke, some in the Old Norse tongue and then repeated in English so we could all share.

I moved through the crowd, greeting and hugging, talking and laughing. Later in the early evening, Alfred, grandad's friend, manoeuvred my wheelchair through the crowd and further down the lawn to the small jetty where Grandad's yacht had been converted into a longboat. His coffin was onboard, secured to the hull and covered in dry wood shavings from his workshop. The yacht had been stripped of the usual winches, stays, halyards and sails. The boom had been moved to the top of the mast and centred there. A large square sail was now attached to it, hung from the top and held there by a few ties. A gentle offshore breeze tugged at the rigging and the ties that held the sail.

"Your grandad is going to Valhalla," Alfred said. "This is what he wanted, we all need to embrace that, to understand how important this was to him."

He turned away for a few moments and his shoulders shook, then slowly turned back to face me. He had tears in his eyes. "And to your grandma too." Alfred then stood tall, lifted a large Gjallarhorn to his lips and blew a long mournful note. The crowd moved down the lawn and gathered at the jetty. We watched as the lines from the jetty and the ties on the sail were released. With a gentle push from four Norsemen the longboat sailed slowly away from the shore, the tiller braced to keep it on course.

I turned to find Grandma, to be with her, but couldn't see her anywhere in the crowd. "Bestomer, Bestomer," I called, but there was no reply. In a panic, I propelled my wheelchair up the lawn, onto the ramp and into the house. Grandma was not there.

A large envelope with my name on it was propped up on the kitchen table. I tore it open, two sealed letters addressed to me, and a single sheet of note paper fell out. All the note said was, "This is now your home, our sweet barnebarn."

14

I spun my wheelchair and propelled it back down the lawn to the jetty. The longboat was well out to sea. Two archers fired flaming arrows in a high arc into the air and they both landed on the boat. It burst into flames that leapt high into the night sky. I grabbed my crutches, staring at the sight, and stood on the wharf, watching the flames devour the ship. A surge of sadness crashed over me, and tears slid down my cheeks as I gazed at the burning vessel.

"Oh, Grandma, Bestomer, what have you done? What have you done?"

Jump, jump

Soleil and Ben are two of only a handful of earthlings with the ability to teleport. They jump to an exoplanet called Amanzi, where there is water, but no plants. When they experiment with pyrophytic plants, trying to create a new ecosystem on the planet, the planet reacts.

About the author: Elizabeth Viljoen
Elizabeth Viljoen is a student of literature who immigrated from Namibia to Auckland. She is working on her first novel, a family saga, and is doing a PhD in mythography. Previously, she was the editor of a small online magazine called *Luhambo | Journey*. Read more on https://northshorewriters.co.nz/our-core-members. Academic writing: https://www.academia.edu/68273022/Die_spelende_mens_in_KLIMTOL_Etienne_van_Heerden_AFSTANDE_Dan_Sleigh_en_SIRKUSBOERE_Sonja_Loots_ Luhambo | Journey online magazine: https://luhambo.wordpress.com/

"Stranded," I whispered, covering my eyes that teared up from the smoke. Billowing – white, grey, black. "Almost."

Ben and I stood on the wharf we constructed last time we were here, about a year ago, watching the flames devour the ship. It was a controlled fire. Planned. Testing our theory. But still.

"I too prefer the old ways of travelling."

"Not cars."

"No, not cars." Ben put his hand on my shoulder. It slipped. Sweat. From the heat. Was that why Jake could not pull Lily from the wreckage? No, do not dwell on the past.

He coughed and drew the neck gaiter over his nose. "Gosh. Nasty sting. We should move farther away." His hand got stuck in the crook of my arm because my body begged to stay. "*Now*."

I turned. Twice. Looking at the walls of the enormous cavern, the water gushing out the fracture at the back. Then my body followed him. Followed his atoms, as they disappeared and reappeared half a mile downriver.

Our coughing surprised me. Was it the smoke we inhaled back there, or did the soot particles follow our atoms? I couldn't remember coughing when I escaped from Jake's car wreck. Although, to be honest, I couldn't remember escaping. Just panicking and suddenly being in my bed at home, under the sheets. I thought I'd woken up from a nightmare, but then felt my hands throb with pain. Severe burns. The dreadful smell of scorched hair. *My* scorched hair. The news said one person, female, was still missing after a vehicle from the Department of Agriculture, Forestry and Fisheries got caught in a veldfire.

Ben pointed to the shaft we dug through the glass-like ceiling to the surface of the planet. "The chimney works well."

"A tick for one part of the theory." The colour of the subterranean river was changing. The stars above turned red.

"We are still way ahead of the team at Oxford," he said and walked to the gear we left on a ledge against the wall of the cavern.

"It's not a competition." My breathing was heavier than usual. There was water around my feet, rising rapidly.

"Su…"

We grabbed the gear and leapt to our small spacecraft on the surface.

"Damn it." Ben hammered his fist on the control panel, just missing the square that would start the ship. His hand flew into the air, hovering, gesturing an apology to the panel.

I smiled. As if the panel had a mind to understand the gesture! "No, Ben, maybe it worked. But the oxygen level will be too low now. And we didn't expect the water to rise. We'll come back in a few months to see if any of the plants took."

He steered the spacecraft over the surface of Amanzi, an exoplanet first observed by Dr Ndaba from the MeerKAT project team in the Northern Cape Province of South Africa. She named it after the Zulu and Xhosa word for water. We checked the opening of the underground tunnel, there where I first travelled eight years ago, but the slow-flowing water was still clear. Well, another check. In Earth time, we calculated, it would take a few hours until the debris and seeds drifted to that point. From there it would spread, following the three distributaries. We landed the spacecraft above the opening where the subterranean river surfaced; positioned the rover and its cameras so that we could monitor the spread of the

19

seeds downstream. We had six more installations to do, then we could return home.

Ben made a fancy nosedive with the spacecraft, skimming over the water. And then it happened. Water busted through the opening of the tunnel, engulfing the spacecraft. The force sent us tumbling. Ben knocked his head on the panel to his right and lost consciousness.

It took all my willpower not to escape. I wouldn't leave a helpless person behind a second time. Stay, *stay*, I willed. I folded my arms over my head in protection.

When we stopped tumbling, one look told me that Ben might be dead. Or that he needed far better medical attention than I could give him. The panels lit up, which meant the craft still worked. We were miles down the river, near a mountain. I landed the craft high up on a flat service, wrapped my arms around Ben, and prayed that we'd both leap in one piece with solely my ability to teleport.

"What the heck!" said Rorisang, my best school friend and the doctor who treated my third-degree burns after I transported from the burning car that first time. She took Ben from my embrace, positioned him on the examination table, and started resuscitating him. In between she scolded. "What if I had a patient in here?"

Then she'd have had two patients to resuscitate. "Miracles happen. I wasn't even sure we'd get here. Come on, Ben. Breathe."

Suddenly he disappeared.

"You'll have to join the British team." Rorisang tried to talk some sense into my head. Her doctor's practice, now transformed into a laboratory, still looked more like a medieval Arab library. Dark bookshelves filled with leatherbound books and scrolls, a colourful mosaic wall, latticed windows, an ancient Persian carpet—inherited from her great-grandmother—on the floor.

"Could you not find anyone else with this gene?"

"There is one other person in our database, but she is not interested in this kind of work."

"Can't we just wait for Ben to recover?"

"Yes, but it may take months." Her hand got stuck in her dark curls. She probably worked through the night, again. "Or years. He keeps disappearing and we don't yet know where he goes."

At least they finally established the medical unit for Project Amanzi. My luck that Rorisang could not use her consultation room for anyone else with Ben in a state of flux.

"Who is the person in the database?"

"Why don't you want to work with the British?"

They didn't need to know. It was personal. At least I no longer cried over him when the owl hooted in the oak below my bedroom window. I bit my lip and frowned.

"Su, she's a lawyer. Don't even try."

"No, I won't. I was just curious."

Rorisang grabbed my hand. "Soleil. *No.*"

I smiled and flicked her hand away. And went back to her lab later that night, to get the address. The lawyer's home and work address.

With a little digging, I found a worthy cause Bettina would love to defend. She did. There was a patch of land near Vermont earmarked for development. The only place where a still to be named blue ghost orchid grew. We won. With information nobody would have been able to discover unless they could sneak in and out of office buildings without being noticed. Only five of us in the world had that ability. Only we and the science teams we worked with knew about this – and were sworn to secrecy.

I lifted my glass of sparkling wine. "I know how you won the case."

We went for drinks to celebrate, very late on the evening after the verdict. She first had to see another client who had a breakdown, until ten. I paid him to freak out for hours.

"Yes, with thorough research. And we had the law on our side. That is why I love defending causes for which I care deeply."

The bar was empty, except for two lonely men, half asleep at the counter, and the bartender. He turned to pour a drink. I emptied my glass; grabbed Bettina's shoulders with both hands. The trick I learned when I rescued Ben.

Next moment we materialised in her office.

She shoved me away. Clutched her tummy. Gagged. Scratched her face.

I waited.

"I *knew* there were others like me, but..."

I raised my brows and folded my arms.

"Have you been... how do you even... why... why do you jump to other planets?"

I smiled. She *knew*. Not all—until now she didn't know that this client of hers was one of the teleporters—but enough. "Only one. An exoplanet. And it was by accident. I was invited to a tour of the new MeerKAT facilities by a friend." Wait. Rorisang. Could she have been...? No. Not Rorisang. But. Why have I never thought of that possibility? She was, after all, the only one who knew, after treating my wounds. No. She wouldn't. Would she?

Bettina didn't say a word. Just nodded. And tilted her head.

"One moment I was fascinated by the stars and exoplanets. The recent discovery of one that might be habitable because there was water. The next moment I was on the planet. Didn't even know it was possible.

"Yes, I freaked out. Couldn't breathe until I realised it was a panic attack and not a lack of oxygen.

"When I returned, the scientists couldn't help themselves. Too many possibilities suddenly opened.

I was just glad we're not Americans! Imagine. They'd put me in a cage, like a lab rat."

Bettina hmphed. "That's the *movies*, not real life. But they *might* have asked you to become a spy."

"And that's not like the movies? Besides, it *is* more or less what you do."

"I defend the innocent! That's different." Was that a smile?

"It is an unfair advantage."

"For the good side."

"I wouldn't say the axe murder case was the good side."

"There are things you don't know about that case. But I'm not at liberty to discuss it." She looked out over the city. The streets that never slept but slowed down. Taillights lit up here and there, small dots on a screen, not a rushed snake hunting for prey like early in the evening.

"What do you want from me?"

"I need a partner, someone to teleport with me."

She whistled, shook her head. "But I'm not interested in science."

"You protected the rare blue ghost orchid."

"It wasn't about biology, it was..."

"About sustainable life on the planet."

"People need houses too."

"But if that side won, we would have lost the blue ghost orchid."

"You are changing an ecosystem too!"

Ha! She knew even that. Who gave her all this information? "It is an experiment. On a habitable planet with no plants or animals."

24

"Which may have repercussions."

"Yes." I slinked down on the leather sofa. "Never thought nature would behave so differently to what we knew. I thought laws that applied here would also apply there."

She turned her back to the window, leaned against the cold glass. "Why not work with the British?"

"You know far more than you let on."

"Your team of scientists has been trying to convince me for over a year now. Each on their own, not telling the others."

"Since Ben came back."

"A little longer. *They* are more worried about the ethical consequences than you are."

"But why don't you want to join? It is the opportunity of a lifetime."

"For you, yes. But not for me. Why don't you come and help me solve cases?"

"Aren't you in the least curious? Only four people in the whole world had been on an exoplanet. And only five have the ability to go. Or go *just like that*. Others will have to wait for technology to catch up and that can be decades from now, even centuries if you consider the travelling time."

"No."

"It will be like going on holiday. To France or the Great Wall of China. Come on, it's just a visit."

"I'm from a dying town in the Karoo. Living in Cape Town was all I ever wanted to do. To be back in District Six, to buy back our family house, from which my grandparents were displaced and..."

"But imagine...!"

"Why do you want me to go with you? Do you need someone to hold your hand?" Was it a racist thing, I thought. Was it because of my light skin? Surely, we have moved beyond that. It was never an issue for Ben. For a moment I wanted to tell her about Nana and her half-sister.

"It is too risky to go alone. Look what happened to Ben."

"All the more reason for me not to go. I cannot understand why you won't join the Oxford team."

"They are so slow. Too cautious."

"You are too much of a risk taker, Soleil. I'm not putting my life in your hands."

Damn. Damn it. Well... "Will you find your way home on your own?"

"I've done it for years."

I stepped forward to hug her, but she ducked away. "Whoa, girl. You broke the code."

"The code has not been written yet."

"Then I'll have to get started."

I smiled, a little awkward, and jumped home to my cosy fourth-floor apartment. The owl's eerie hoot welcomed me. What could I do? I fell onto the couch, sulked. Climbed into bed, turned and turned and turned. And turned. Tossed the duvet off, walked out onto the balcony, slumped down, almost missing the deck chair, sighed, stared into space. Shut up, I whispered to the owl. If only Ben could stabilise. I longed to go to the water place. Yes, that's what I'd do. Go to Amanzi. On my own. Fearless. On Monday. Yes, or the day after.

I closed my eyes. Saw the underground cathedral where we lit up the ship. Or boat. An old wooden fishing vessel. It was an accomplishment getting it there. Ben and I practised for weeks, teleporting it from Cape Town to Auckland to Marseille to Puerto Vallarta and back to Cape Town at hours nobody would notice. We felt like kids in a secret society.

The light shimmered through the ceiling of the cavern, turned the stalactites a sparkling blue, the water pink and purple and orange. Water bubbled up, from deep inside the planet.

Birds chirped, large butterflies fluttered, a man's voice called out, "*Su*, finally!"

What a lovely dream. A Persian cat was sprawled out on a rug at Ben's feet. A slightly older Ben. He sat in a rocking chair, dropping the orange he was peeling. He rushed to me, hugged me so tight that it felt like a real hug.

I mumbled in his sleeve. "I can't wait for you to stabilise so that we can meet in real life."

He coughed, shook his head. "What do you mean, Soleil? I've been travelling back and forth for decades, bringing over fruit trees and birds and insects and old Grumpy here. Even furniture. This is real." He pinched my arm.

"Ouch!" I flicked away his fingers.

But he grabbed my arm tighter and pulled me in the direction of an orchard. "We've been waiting for *you* to come out of the coma after you rescued me. Your body kept disappearing."

27

"No, Ben. It was *you* who kept disappearing. You were knocked unconscious when the river attacked us."

"The river didn't attack us."

"Yes, it did."

"Are you saying the river has a will of its own? I have never experienced anything like that in the decades since I returned."

I turned him around to see the yellowing of the river, but it changed back as soon as he looked in that direction. He shrugged, then patted me on the back. Smiling, but frowning.

"Come, there is someone I want you to meet. My wife. She is one of us. Bettina, darling, come look, you would never guess who is here."

We climbed two flights of stone stairs to the house cave they dug out of the cavern wall. Bettina was arranging a vase of proteas. "Soleil! What a miracle." She walked around the large wooden dining room table in the front room. "These are from the pioneer seeds you and Ben sent down the stream."

I reached out to hug her, but she took a step back. "Hugs are against the code."

Something's Onboard

Capt. James Hurst, a young British army surgeon, is seen as cursed and subsequently dispatched to the colonies in the hope of being well rid of him. Onboard the ship he meets a young research assistant, and an unlikely romance begins. That is, until the vessel picks up some mysterious shipwreck survivors…

About the author: Andrew Imms
Andrew Imms has been a consultant, a fencing coach, an actor, and a company director. He has survived his own and the stupidity of others narrowly many times, danced naked in a church, and spent the night singing in Istanbul in the rain. He writes oddball thrillers and weird horror.

Ship's log under the command of Captain William Baines, Her Majesty's British Navy, Wednesday, November 23rd, 1859.

Record of the miscellaneous events of the day.

Entry by Captain James Hurst of the 12th East Suffolk Foot Infantry.

You may choose to believe this or not. It doesn't matter, but I swear it is the living truth, so help me God … as if the Lord could help me now.

I write this not in contrition, but I need to … no … I *have* to … get this down in writing, for my own sanity, such as it is, after these dreadful occurrences.

It was the year of our lord 1859. As I marched up the boarding plank and onto the quarter deck of the HMS Varnae in Calcutta, I could already feel something was off.

As an English gentleman, I promptly ignored it, of course.

Varnae was a three-mast sloop of war, apparently fifth rate, the crew told me, whatever the dickens that meant, but more than enough to handle pirates or worse, the French, with or without the five score of able seamen on board.

Naval vessels are normally teeming, and everywhere you turn you are at risk of tripping over a boatswain or a cooper or some form of midshipman. Varnae, on the other hand, had only a couple of dozen sailors working on the main deck, and there was none of the nonstop shouting, singing, and swearing I was accustomed to. The British army teaches you not to enquire about such things, besides it was none of my business, as I was just a passenger, so I kept my mouth shut.

My orders were taking me down to New Zealand, where I was to be joining the 12th Suffolk Infantry as the regimental surgeon. The Suffolk had been sent down to settle some issue with apparently restless natives. After serving at the behest of her majesty for quite some time, I'd seen this sort of thing before. One or more private companies had no doubt double-crossed the natives, and the British Army were there to defend against the theft of land.

Honestly, it didn't matter to me either way—I just wanted somewhere to disappear.

The reassignment was purely political, of course. You see, I'm seen as cursed by Army command; you know—ill luck to have around.

It all started with the death of my wife Heather and my boys from the consumption while I was off fighting Nickolas the Bloody. I'm afraid that's where my mind cracked, and my faith failed.

No … that's a falsehood.

At the Siege of Sevastopol, after sawing off yet another young man's limb, I made the mistake of taking a breath and looked up at the abject horror. Through the clouds of flies and across the blood-stained snow, I took in all the deaths from cholera, the musket, the bayonet, the Russian winter, but mostly the gross stupidity of the British commanding officers, ordering little more than children to their deaths with no modicum of strategy or plan.

I thought, *What God could allow this?* I decided right then and there that God didn't give a damn about us. Therefore, I would take it upon myself.

That's when the alarming series of coincidences which led to the deaths of many senior officers around me started. There were the usual side glances, hushed whispers, and that sort of thing. Superstitious fools, the lot of them.

I, of course, had murdered every damn last one of them. Some quite inventively, I must say.

Obviously, being a doctor, I had access to many drugs and chemicals, so I started with poisoning. I enjoyed the irony when I was called in to treat the very same affliction I had caused.

Too many poisonings would of course have drawn suspicion, so I then moved to an obvious murder, incriminating another officer whom I also disliked. Two birds with one stone approach, or in this case two birds with one brutal stabbing in the night. When the second party got off the charges a crude explosive charge rolled into their tent in the dead of night, giving the impression of retribution done by some aggrieved friend. Case closed.

From there things became even more elaborate. All the classic novelist murders were included in my resumé. A fake suicide, a tent catching fire in the night, and a drunken flapdoodle—who thought we were meeting some local farmer's daughters, only to be pushed off a cliff. His confused countenance still brings a smile to my face.

Be not concerned about the unpleasant fate of these men. Trust me—they were commensurate bastards. Nothing could be proven, of course, and needless to say, before you could say Jack Robinson, I was shipped off to New Zealand in the express hope I would never be seen or heard from again.

You may ask why on earth I would put this down in ink, freely and without reservation.

As you read on, you will see my previous misdeeds pale in comparison to what has transpired here.

The trip for me started fine, as I kept to my berth and spent most of my time reading, accompanied by my mistress—a turquoise glass hypodermic syringe. Regrettably, I was expected to share the captain's table in the great cabin, and after evading it for a week, I simply ran out of excuses and was therefore forced to attend. The meal was thoroughly unremarkable, but what happened was not.

I hadn't formally met any of the other passengers on board, so there was a string of tedious introductions.

Greeting me first was the ship's Captain, William Baines, your stereotypical Scotsman with his mutton chops, deep brogue, and a red nose from too much whiskey. As the conversation wore on, I would learn that apparently the joy of sharing the captain's table is to hear him go on and on about "bloody darkies," which got louder as the night went on and he consumed more liquor.

Firstly, a tall man to the left of the captain stood and banged his head on the ceiling as he attempted to shake hands. Beside him was probably his wife, whom he completely forgot to introduce. She was indeed lovely and reminded me of my Heather, even down to her flaxen hair. The memory was like a dagger to my heart.

Geoffery Winterbottom informed me almost immediately, and then repetitively throughout the evening, that he had bought huge tracts of land south of the city of Auckland, where he intended to farm. It would be fair to describe him as the sort of man who seemed to have a cricket stump well and truly shoved up their bottom. Eventually, he presented his wife Cora, who asked if I had a wife and family back in England.

I find it best to lie in those situations. It's easier on everyone.

"What are you doing in New Zealand?" a new voice enquired. The man introduced himself as Samuel Sweet, an Anglican vicar who was travelling to a parish in the Waikato and had high hopes of bringing the natives to God. He was a plain man in every sense of the word.

In response to his inquiry, I informed him, "Probably sending the very same natives to hell on behalf of rich farmers like Mr Winterbottom here."

After that, people stopped asking me questions.

Continuing around, I was seated at the foot of the table. For your benefit, I would presume to describe myself as having a moderately good-looking countenance, tallish with a well-kept moustache, but in a dishevelled officer's uniform. I used to have kind eyes. I don't know what they are anymore.

Chin up and chest puffed out like a prize bantam, was a supposedly renowned naturalist and geologist, Professor George Warner.

"Pleased to make your acquaintance Captain," he stated, presenting an overly enthusiastic handshake. "I was just elaborating on the importance of my exploration for the Royal geological society, and some of the most incredible discoveries the Society and I have been doing into furthering our scientific knowledge. In fact, this very voyage is a result of my expedition, no less. You have me to thank for your free ride, so to speak."

I was about to say something I would no doubt regret, when my train of thought was broken by a young woman standing there beside him and offering me her lace-gloved left hand.

'Yes, this is my niece, Lucy, who is accompanying me to assist with my research,' declared Warner.

I nearly choked on my wine when I heard that.

Warner was short, rotund, in his early forties and already balding. Lucy on the other hand looked to be barely twenty. It was striking that the two women in the room couldn't be any more different. Like two sides of a coin. One was fair, dressed for summer and brought a light to the room, while the other was raven-haired, aquiline, and attired for a funeral. Despite his bluster, Warner wasn't a threat to anyone but the sherry bottle. Lucy, well, that was an entirely different matter.

I'm a truly evil bastard. I'll take that. I can't put it in words, but you just know others … and staring into those piercing eyes, it was not a girl that stared back—but a killer.

Apprehensively I took my seat next to what for all appearances was a perfectly pleasant young woman. I can't recall the conversation at this time, as I was too busy noticing how she playfully ran her fingers up and down the blade of her dinner knife. What I do remember was that I drank far too much wine in an effort to drown my fear.

After an unidentifiable stew, which is indeed saying something considering what I've eaten, Warner proudly broke out a mysterious map covered in writing from damn knows where. I can't say I had much confidence in it, as there seemed to be any number of inaccuracies on it, and pictures of fanciful beasts.

Ungainly, he finished his wine glass in one gulp to wash down what was left of his raspberry summer pudding.

"Ahem. I thought I would present to you what this is all about so to speak. This map was originally obtained by sixteenth-century Portuguese sailors from Malay spice traders and then held in the offices of the VoC for around one hundred and twenty years. It may actually be even older as it's written on silk that, as some of you no doubt know, makes its point of origin in China, probably the Ming dynasty, no less. Which could date it to around the year of our lord fourteen hundred, or perhaps even earlier."

The Professor picked up the captain's map magnifier and, without permission, I might add, placed it on the ancient map. I smiled at the liberty.

"Now, despite the frightful embellishments, you will all see a staggering amount of accuracy, including the greater Indonesia archipelago represented, as well as the west coast of Australia, no less. Here we even see the Borneo Coral Isles, but what we have also mapped here is this set of islands roughly a thousand nautical miles west of those isles. Ladies and gentlemen, I believe we have found Mount Meru of Kumari Kadam, also known as …the sunken continent of Lemuria."

If he was expecting any reaction, clapping, gasps, he didn't get it.

From the vicar and Mr Winterbottom, he did receive a number of polite, and I might add asinine, follow-up questions. What did come out was that our course would not be through the Malaccas, but instead to this damned uncharted atoll and then to Perth.

I wasn't entirely happy with this state of affairs, as it seemed to me to be a wild goose chase—and I would have preferred a few days in Singapore to being lost in the southern Indian Ocean looking for a rock that didn't exist. Regrettably, since I'd drunk far too much wine, I may have unconsciously said as much out loud.

Rather than Warner responding, it was however young Lucy—which, I need to add, she did seamlessly while placing a hand on my leg under the table.

"Don't worry, I think we can find something to keep you occupied."

It wasn't the forwardness that concerned me (frequenting brothels was somewhat of a hobby of mine); it was that I now noticed everyone hanging off her words. It was as if she held them all in the palm of her hand, and when she finished speaking it faded like the tide going out. Damnedest thing.

Oh, that—and her hand.

Her touch was so cold, I wondered for a moment if she were alive. Spending time in Crimea, I was used to women stealing my warmth, but not like this. Not wanting to cause a scene, my only option was to sit there and pretend nothing was happening. I fear this only increased her mischievous nature, as she then started to move her hand up my leg.

In response, I stood up abruptly and, in a fluster, announced, "Ahh... yes... excuse me, everyone, thank you for the dinner and the company, but I seem, well that is, I'm not feeling particularly well, nothing to be concerned about, probably sea sickness or the like, so will make my apologies and retire."

It should also be noted I locked the door of my cabin that night.

The following week was spent doing my darnedest to avoid young Miss Lucy, and as such was generally successful and uneventful.

Except, of course, for three notable occurrences.

First were the whalers we picked up.

There were just three survivors in a whaleboat: the foremast mate, the harpooner, and the first mate. The foremast mate was a swarthy Norwegian, you know the sort; that smelled and looked like a horse, with an unkept mane and a bushy beard, which I wouldn't have been surprised to find ferrets lurking in. The harpooner turned out to be West African, a fat man, black as an ace of spades, with unusual scar tattoos all over his face. At the time I worried about how having a black man on board would go down with Baines, and whether I would need to intercede. But the third man placated any concerns I might have had about the safety of the African man.

First mate Erasmus Järtlös looked like he had come straight out of Beowulf, ominous and terrible. The brutally handsome man was well over six and a half feet, and stared down at the crew in the same way as an eagle would to its quarry. He was obviously of an unkind heart and not to be trifled with, but for all his foreboding that's not what I noticed.

It was his woollen greatcoat. You see, Heather and I had resided in Westminster for a time, and would often walk down Saville Row on the way to

Burlington Gardens for the children to play in. As such, I'm quite familiar with fine-tailored coats, and the coat this man was wearing was definitely not what you would see on a sailor. The huge lapels, the velvet and the fine wool, made it more of something you would see on an English lord on a hunting trip in Scotland. I wondered how this fellow had come upon such a fine garment.

Subsequently, I chanced to overhear, and by that, I mean I eavesdropped, that their ship, the Magnus, apparently hit something in a storm, and they made it to one of the boats and had been at sea for quite some time.

I remember thinking how similar this was to the plot of an American novel about a whale I had just read last week. Curiouser and curiouser.

The next event was—well, at the time it wasn't significant, but looking back now, I see its importance.

I regret to say that I started to have the most inappropriate dreams about young Miss Lucy. The things that happened in these dreams, well, they were not something a gentleman puts to paper, but let's just say the dreams were vivid. Most vivid. So much so that when I awoke, I would find myself drenched in perspiration and more fatigued than when I went to bed. Worse, I found myself becoming wearier and wearier after each night. I'm ashamed to say while my state in the morning was worrisome, that didn't stop me from continuing to self-administer Laudanum in the evenings. Not in the slightest.

Finally, there was the fog.

My experiences of fog were never pleasant. In London it is malodorous and yellow; in Crimea, it was mixed with the sulphur of black powder and the rotting stench of death.

This fog appeared from nowhere and rolled in like the 4:20 into Paddington, covering us all in a cool mist and blocking out the hot sun. Surprisingly, I thought at the time how lovely it was, reminding me of my childhood in Kent. The sailors, being superstitious, only found it disturbing, remarking that it was unnatural, a bad omen and other such nonsense. Over the next few days, however, their opinions gained weight when it just didn't go away, and the accompanied behaviour of the crew began to change, as they became somnolent, muttering to themselves, or just standing there and staring off into the fog at seemingly nothing.

Now that I look back, I realise they were all staring off in the same direction.

It was not only the crew but also the passengers whose behaviour started to change. The conversation had become quite peculiar now, to say the least, as if a great weight bore down on everyone. Whenever I chanced to see Captain Baines, he seemed to be

41

fending off innumerable enquiries about the damn fog.

"*Aye, aye, it will pass soon,*" or "*Don't be daft, laddie, this often happens in the Southern Ocean.*"

Only this wasn't the Southern Ocean…

I received several friendly overtures from Mr Winterbottom to join himself and his wife Cora for an evening of cards in their cabin. They were most enthusiastic, explaining that they played both bridge and canasta and had a bottle of Mother's Ruin stashed away. Normally I'd have been game, free alcohol and all, but they were a little too friendly, if you know what I mean, so I was fairly certain it was some ruse to get me drunk and then into some perverted boarding class ménage à trois.

There was also the difficulty with the Professor. On walks around the ship, Warner started to deliberately steer Miss Lucy away from me or would position his body between us to block any form of exchange. You would think that I would have been thankful for this, and to some extent I was, but I also saw the opportunity for sport.

As I said, I'm a bastard.

Upon seeing the two of them, I always made a point of making a greeting, directly addressing Miss Lucy to enquire as to how her day was, in front of her 'uncle', and would sit back and watch for the reaction from him. It was utterly tremendous seeing the jealousy set fire to his face.

Niece my arse…

However, all of this was quite different from the interactions between Master Järtlös and Miss Lucy.

Järtlös had been given free access to the entire ship, for some curious reason, despite the fact he was a foreigner, and seemed to turn up all over the place. I didn't have a problem with this, as the man, while a touch haughty, was generally amenable to all.

Except, however, for Miss Lucy.

What I observed was that he and Miss Lucy appeared to be not on speaking terms and seemed to be actively avoiding each other. This didn't make sense—there was no way the two of them could have been acquainted. But regardless, the polite animosity was there for all to see. On the rare occasion that one or both of them couldn't graciously retire, I swear their posture reminded me of two feral cats in a standoff.

All of this paled in comparison, when on the fifth day I began to notice something that gave me great reason to be concerned. Uniformly there was a paleness in the visage of my fellow passengers. This could be many things: a lack of meat, vegetables, the damn fog blocking out the sun, but one possibility terrified me.

The consumption.

If it was on board, and this had indeed become a plague ship, this would not go well.

No ... not at all.

We were God-knows-where in the Indian Ocean, and the standard treatment was cocaine and opium to ease the symptoms. Well, let's just say, there are far fewer stocks than when we set out, and would not be enough for the passengers, let alone the crew.

I began to wonder if perhaps my fitful dreams were a warning sign, so I decided it was best to continue with my usage—as a treatment now, you understand.

On the sixth day of fog, I heard a most enchanting ballad coming from up top, and using the device of taking a constitutional pipe of tobacco, I threw on my smoking jacket and headed out upon the quarter-deck to see where it was coming from.

"My love, my darling, who forsook me at the altar,
I shall not, nay will not, be seen to falter.
I watch her, I follow her, way down to the river,
My throat dries, my hands shake, and I try not to quiver."

As I made it to the top of the stairs, it was the horrendous rank that hit me first, and I was instantly pulled back to the field hospital at Balaclava. The screaming, the flies, the smell of burnt flesh and gangrene.

"A twig snaps, it's so loud, how could she not hear,

44

My breath held, and my heart pounds, I'd
gotten so near.

I rush her, my last chance, but find only dismay,
A knife glints, and she grins wide, turns out I'm
the prey."*

The song pulled me back from the brink, and I
headed in the direction of the music; and there on the
forecastle was young Lucy, white pinafore covered in
blood, singing, and smiling gleefully. She had already
opened the abdomen of a huge seabird and was in the
process of pulling out its guts into a bucket with a
heavy wet plop. I must have looked like a fool as I
stood there gaping as she proceeded to press her
thumbs under the feathers and then with a clean
action pulled back the skin like one would peeling an
orange.

With a practised grace, if dismembering
animals had a grace, that is, the skin was swiftly
stretched and tacked on a board, and then she began
to effortlessly debone the carcass. Only then did she
look up, in my direction of course, and while
enveloped with buzzing flies presented a wide toothy
grin.

I physically choked, before regathering my
equilibrium, and began to make a judicious retreat.

Only I noticed something move out of the
corner of my eye. It disappeared behind the foremast,
near the galley stove cowl.

I recall reasoning that I had simply imagined it,
or more likely it was the ship's cat or merely a rat,

45

and to forget it. But for the life of me I just couldn't, and unconsciously in time to Lucy's singing, I started to move towards where it was.

"I see that she had me, all the time at her ease,
My blood flows, my heart stops, and I fall to my knees."

Bit by bit, I crept closer, holding my breath, and as I approached the corner, for some inexplicable reason, I leapt around to surprise whatever it was.

But oddly there was nothing there to be seen.

Absolutely nothing.

About then I felt the strangest feeling and looked up to my right to see, off in the distance, Järtlös staring straight at me. It was an odd stare, almost as if he were sizing me up, and then without so much as a *by your leave*, he just turned and walked away.

Captain Baines approached me on the evening of the seventh day of fog.

It appeared that, before I put on board, something untoward had happened with their ship's surgeon, about which I found Baines somewhat vague. As a result, they had been operating with only a surgeon's mate fulfilling the role for some time. Regrettably, the gentleman performing the role, Master Bowers, had been taken down with an affliction, and Baines requested if I could check on him. This afforded a great opportunity to rifle through the ship's supplies, so I accepted, of course.

Immediately upon entering the sick bay, I became concerned. The gentleman, Bowers, seemed to be slipping in and out of consciousness and was shockingly emaciated, as if something was sucking the very life from him. The man was as cold as the grave, but still sweating as if he had a fever, all of which made no sense at all. Added to this, his other symptoms were pallor, lethargy, and loss of appetite.

Then I observed something even more puzzling.

I had just unbuttoned his shirt, so as to listen to his chest with my stethoscope, when I noticed something was amiss with his throat. There was light blue bruising all the way around it as if he'd had a trip to the gallows, and a weeping wound about the size of a guinea coin on one side. I had never seen it's like before. My best guess was that it might have been a combination of an infected animal bite, jaundice, or perhaps goitre, but honestly, I had no idea. It was all terribly worrisome.

I cleaned and bandaged the wound and then administered a dose of laudanum from my own stock to quieten him down. Once he was stable, and more importantly asleep, I went through his pockets, looking for the key to the dispensary next door, with the express intention to restock my own.

In the British Army, you literally have to tie things down to prevent theft. When one happened to forget to lock things up, or was simply looking the

47

other way, it was very common for enlisted men to purloin anything, but especially the ethanol. I'm not sure of Naval protocols, but I was fairly certain it would be common practice, so you would understand my surprise to find the dispensary door unlocked.

The room appeared to be in disarray; either there had been an altercation in there or, more likely, someone had ransacked it.

As the sick bay directly backed onto the crew berth deck, and was only separated from view by sheets, I spun around to see if I was being observed. All I could see in the dim light through fluttering sheets were the crew hammocks. Dozens upon dozens of them, suspended from the roof. I recalled a school trip to some local caverns as a child, where some of us absconded off to explore the caves as a dare. There, we came across a chamber filled to the brim with what I believe now to have been greater horseshoe bats. The others ran for it, of course, but I just stood there astonished, marvelling at the colony as they roosted, hanging there from the roof. A lot like the crew I now watched.

An odd memory to return, I thought.

Entering the room, I got about my business, opening cupboards to see if anything had been left behind. I was about halfway through, and not having much success, I might add, when I thought I heard something. So slight was the noise, I wasn't entirely sure that I had heard anything at all. If I had to describe it, I would hazard to say perhaps a scratching or perchance a scraping coming from one of the cabinets.

Of course, the noises, imagined or not, had come from one cabinet in particular—larger than the rest and made of solid oak with a large, rusted padlock on it.

I scoured through the unlocked alcoves, but found nothing of value, while all the time keeping an eye on that one locker.

Eventually, I had finished looking through all the other cabinets and found myself standing there in front of the locked cabinet, with no excuse not to open it. Hesitantly I looked down at the large key to the lock, at the ornate bow, and I couldn't shake the feeling that it was shaped like an eye. An eye that was looking back at me.

"Get a grip man," I exclaimed out loud, reasoning that I was overreacting and that by actually vocalising I could drive away the dark clouds of fear.

Slowly and carefully, I inserted the long blade of the key into the lock and turned it. There was a heavy click but then nothing. I stood there confused when without warning there was a loud crack, and the lock fell open. It only then occurred to me that I'd neglected to breathe for quite a while, so after a few inhalations, and feeling a bit better, I decided there was nothing to worry about. I recall my mouth curved into a smile—as the crew's theft had afforded me the perfect opportunity to blame them for the disappearance of anything I found inside this cabinet.

I slid the shackle out from the cabinet bracket and began to open the door, when it burst open by itself, and inside, a hissing and snarling black shape lunged at me, attempting to slice me with its sharp claws.

The ship's cat had somehow been locked in, and the hellion bolted past me at blinding speed and out the door. I stood there for God knows how long, recovering from the shock and hoping I wasn't about to die from angina pectoris. As I stood there in silence, I wondered why on earth someone would lock a cat in a cabinet. Was it a prank? Or perhaps some maliciousness towards the poor animal. It was then in the stillness I could have sworn I heard something else moving in the darkened corner of the room.

But there was nothing in that space…

It was a sliding sound, like leather on wood, but oh so quiet, as you would think you imagined it. There I stood, gaping at the darkness from whence the sound came, and saw absolutely nothing, just a shadow.

But then, to my horror, the shadow itself shifted.

The hairs on my arm went up, followed by goosebumps. My breath shortened, and I went cold in dread. A thousand thoughts went through my mind, but one came out clear. *Run.*

I snapped up my medical bag, not even taking time to close it, and, following the cat's lead, immediately made it for the door, slamming it shut behind me as I went. I fumbled around in my pockets, eventually finding the keys, and despite my hands trembling, locked the dispensary door behind me. Not stopping there, I bolted up the stairs until I was topside and grabbed the rail, whereupon, doubled over, I took some deep breaths and attempted to regain my equilibrium.

About now I thought of Bowers in the next room. Had I abandoned him to the shade's mercy? Now, with distance and the clarity of fresh air, I reasoned that it surely must have all been a trick of the light and the ship making odd noises. From a self-diagnosis point of view, the most likely explanation was actually that I was now suffering waking delirium, so he was in no danger except from that odd wound. Of course, there was a third choice, but let's just say to give in to those thoughts led to madness or worse. Anyway, I determined to check on him first thing in the morning, regardless of my fear.

When I finally recovered enough composure to raise my head, I peered up to see if anyone had observed my irrational conduct. Thankfully no one seemed to have noticed my discomfort, or if they had been politely ignoring me. I was not sure if this was a good or a bad thing.

I must add, however, that rather than someone, something, was indeed watching me.

Looking down at me from one of the deck boats was that damned cat, and I could have sworn for the life of me the bloody thing smiled at me.

Later that evening I did, however, report to Captain Baines my concerns about not only Bowers and the dispensary theft, but also the troubling behaviour I had seen across the entire crew.

I neglected to mention anything else, of course.

Baines was a large man and was supporting his weight by leaning on the map table, looking down and avoiding my gaze. However, the more I spoke, the more I could see his white knuckles as his hands firmly clenched the edges of the table. It was hard to tell if he was steading himself or about to fly into a fit of rage.

"And you are sure it's the consumption?" he asked in an aggressive tone.

Rather than inflame the man, I decided to calm things down before they became unseemly.

"It's too early to say. The good news is that I haven't heard the persistent cough. It's a particular sound, rasping with white phlegm which is damn hard to miss. What we could have is some form of ship-wide infection, or something perhaps diet related. Either way, I thought it prudent to bring it to your attention, as it may need keeping an eye on so to speak?"

He finally looked up and met my eyes. What I recognised was a visage I was far too well acquainted with. It was the same look I got from telling men I was about to cut a limb off. Stoic stiff upper lip, but really just a façade. Obviously, this was disquieting— as this was a hardened sailor who had seen combat numerous times. If he was worried, that meant things were worse than I imagined.

"That will be all, Captain Hurst."

At the time I was torn between relief that it was someone else's problem; irked at the nerve of the man simply dismissing me; and concerned that he wasn't really going to follow up.

Were we all about to be pulled into a mutiny, or a plague, or perhaps both?

It was the next morning when it hit me like a bullet to the forehead.

Master Bowers was up and walking around.

First thing, after a standard breakfast of a cup of tea and some weevil-infested bread, I went to check on him in sick bay. Only he wasn't there. Concerned that he might have perished in the night, I asked a passing sailor, who just sheepishly pointed to the dispensary.

The door was open, and there were sounds coming from inside.

After swallowing my distress, I gingerly peered into the room past the open door, and there was Master Bowers, fully dressed and ensconced in tidying up the room. He saw me, turned, and gave me a naval salute.

"Damn cat got in 'ere again and made an 'ell of a mess. Next time I sees it, I gonna wring its scrawny neck."

Putting on the same stoic face I'd seen Baines show me the previous night, I agreed with him, and told him how happy I was to see him up and about. I even told him not to overdo it before I left him to it.

This was a lie, of course. As I walked away, and he couldn't see me, I went pale. Last night that man was on death's door. He should have been in a burial shroud, not walking around.

I went straight for the captain's bed place.

As I walked along the upper deck, I passed Järtlös casually chatting with the Quartermaster, Holland, I believe the man's name was, and he stopped to give me a morning nod, the type that says *good morning*, but actually is more of an *I see you*. I gave nothing away, giving him a cheery, "Hello," as I passed.

When I arrived at Bain's quarters, however, I found there was a guard on the door and was informed that the captain had been taken ill, and no one was to enter. When I attested that as a surgeon, perhaps I should look at him, the Marine on guard

54

instructed me, "Master Bowers is looking after captain."

I'm not a fool, so I gave him a smile and said, "Righto," and went about my business.

Where some may see coincidence, I saw a conspiracy. About now I also realised I hadn't seen any of the Wardroom officers in days.

This wasn't an infection after all, but malfeasance; but by whom and to what end...?

Retaining a modicum of reason, I did actually understand that my evening dalliances in narcotics meant that I may not be the most dependable judge of the situation, so I thought it judicious to enlist a clearer head into my investigations.

The list of those whom I didn't suspect was quite short, and the list of those who could be trusted even shorter, so I found myself knocking on the door of the vicar, Samuel Sweet. Why the vicar, you may ask? I've found sailors to be a generally superstitious lot, and a man of the cloth is generally to be trusted— nay, revered—and wouldn't be harmed if perchance this all went to hell.

Fortunately, the vicar was surprisingly receptive to my concerns, and agreed to meet me that evening for a clandestine search; in fact, he seemed palpably excited. I don't know what I expected to find: maybe a deranged lunatic had poisoned the food, mutinous sailors, foreign spies, or more likely that I was just paranoid. Regardless, that night I slipped out of my berth and up the stairs to the upper deck. There seemed to be fewer and fewer sailors about every night. I hoped they were in their hammocks sleeping, but suspected something far, far grimmer.

It was after midnight when I caught up to Sweet, at the bow of the upper deck, between the foremast and the manger. Oddly he didn't seem himself, and was now missing the excitement in the task he displayed earlier. In fact, he seemed to be almost maudlin for some unfathomable reason. I, however, was completely at ease after taking a healthy dose of both opium and cocaine before leaving my room. I'd even loaded a syringe with a top-up if need be.

The other reason for my lack of trepidation was that tucked into my jacket pocket was my fully loaded service revolver. You may say to yourself, no good can come from a drug-addled fool with a loaded pistol—and you would be right.

We crept up the stairs, by the belfry onto the quarterdeck, and to the fresh air. This seemed to be the best place to discreetly talk, as in that location we were obscured from sight by the lifeboats, and were far enough away from the wheel for anyone to hear our clandestine plans.

"I've been pondering," I said keeping both my voice and head down. "Perhaps we should undertake to see the captain again. You might divert the attention of the Marine, whilst I slip in?"

His forehead creased in disapproval. "I don't really think I would like to be involved in falsehoods and subterfuge. Besides, what if it goes wrong? No, I believe we need to know more first, and that the answer will most likely lay in the hull."

I wanted to reply, to suggest another action, anything, but fear silenced my tongue. I don't know why, but at the mention of the hull I broke out into a cold sweat. I'd never been to the hull, as officially it was off-limits to the passengers. But was that the real reason I'd never been down there?

As he continued on, my attention was distracted by the feel of the cool night fog on my face. It was as if a lover was gently caressing my cheeks, and as her cold wet fingertips touched my lips, I closed my eyes and breathed deeply as my thoughts swam away into the embrace. Fingertips tingled, and I could have sworn I smelt thick perfume and heard whispers off in the distance, but couldn't quite make out the words.

There was another smell, though, off in the distance that I knew all too well. Something …wrong….

"Captain Hurst, sir, Captain Hurst?"

I'm not sure how long my eyes were shut, but when I finally opened them, I was greeted by Vicar Sweet staring at me as if I was completely off my rocker. Snapping back to reality, I pretended that I had indeed been listening, and agreed that we make it for the hull, and the main hold. I apologized and made the feeble excuse that I wasn't feeling particularly great, while all the time knowing damn full well that I must have "self-medicated" far too much.

This became even more worrisome as we made our way down the steps and the hallucinations really started to kick in.

If you pardon my French, I've taken a hell of a lot of drugs in my life. But I can honestly say I'd never experienced anything like this before.

It was as if the night had come to life and I could see a different world, an unseen world that was always there. It was as if I had been wearing a dark veil and had it removed suddenly, bringing everything into focus.

I followed Samuel as we stole through the ship. To my surprise, the Vicar was remarkably stealthy as we crept back down to the upper deck, or more accurately, the gun deck. We couldn't use the stairs at the bow, as they would take us straight into the middle of the crew berths; therefore we needed to make our way to the stairs near the mainmast.

Stairs that were close to the Marine guarding the captain's bed place.

Despite the ship being mostly open plan, we were out of his direct sight, being blocked by the capstan, the pumps and the wall supporting the stairs.

Unfortunately, however, as I passed row after row of the 12-pounder guns, I started to lose touch with reality, imagining the coldness of the gun-metal grey cylinders.

Never alive, whose only purpose was to take life. Dark tubes of death and destruction.

The good news was that I immediately regained my wits when the Vicar tripped on the edge of the main hatch which was obscured in the darkness. The bad news was that the marine heard him too.

"Who goes there?" challenged the Lance Corporal, as he stood and raised his lantern for a better view.

I didn't give the Vicar a chance to reply.

With one hand I smothered the vicar's mouth, and with the other tucked under the back of his collar I dragged him behind the mainmast looking out for whence the light from the Marines lantern extended.

"Don't you be playing silly buggers with me now. If there is someone there, make yourself be known," he said as he slowly advanced.

To the Vicar, I held a finger to my lips, and began to slip off my boots, and thankfully the Vicar took the hint and followed my lead, also taking off his shoes. I could hear the marine's footsteps coming closer as I grabbed one of the Vicar's oxfords and threw it the length of the ship, landing somewhere near the foremast in the darkness.

Samuel gave me a filthy look at the loss of his shoe.

Happily, this had the desired effect, and the Lance Corporal ran past where we were concealed, which afforded us the opportunity to slink silently down the stairs unseen.

Now on the lower deck, where the berths were, we could use the pump room to hide us from the crew, and in the other direction the ship's pantries, to conceal us if a passenger emerged.

Which of course one did.

The professor, looking decidedly guilty of something untoward, slipped out of his cabin and gently knocked on a door. I wasn't sure whose door that was, but no one opened it. He rapped again, this time firmly, and even at this distance I could see he was palpably enraged. When no one opened, he went to another door, performed an odd tempo knock, and the door seemed to swing open by itself. Whose room this was is unknown to me, and I couldn't see inside, but what I could see didn't make much sense. It was pure darkness, packed so tight that it seemed to overflow out into the hall.

Warner vacillated for a moment before he entered, and the door closed behind him. Now I think about it I can't recall anyone pulling it shut, but there could have been someone in that total blackness. Not that I could tell either way.

Regardless we proceeded down the stairs, farther into the bowels of the ship.

My delirium seemed to get even worse, if that was actually possible, as the hull seemed to transform into a huge oak leaf; beams and framing becoming pulsing veins and venules. My jaw fell open as my sight further altered, and a ghastly blight began to spread from the centre of the ship across the leaf blade like an infection.

As I stepped off the bottom step, I could feel that I was standing in something wet. At first, I thought it was seawater, but it was thick like a treacle. In fact, treacle was a rather good analogy, as it seemed to be mucilaginous as well. Nevertheless, here we were in a cramped passage, which led to many doors. To the aft of the boat, to the steward's room, to the slop room, to the officer's stores, and finally, a large weighty door, which headed to the main hold.

I quivered as I realised the door to the main hold was in the direction the blight emanated from. Even worse, Samuel seemed to be most adamant that we look in there first. He'd even stepped to the door, held the handle, and gestured for me to enter.

I didn't know what was behind that door, but every part of me screamed not to go in there.

As an alternative, I made the excuse that to be thorough we should commence from the aft of the ship, and then spun and directly headed in the opposite direction from the hold. I disappeared through into the filling room and up a couple of stairs finally into the bread room. Predictably, it was simply a large storeroom filled with hard bread, and as far as I could tell held nothing untoward at all. That was until I felt a hand on my shoulder, gently but at the same time firmly, trying to direct me back in the direction of the hold.

"*This way, my son.*"

I turned and saw a smiling Samuel, and the blood drained from my face.

Below his cravat, something moved.

Now that I saw it, I couldn't believe how I couldn't have seen it before. From its outline, it was like an adder or an eel, shifting and winding about his neck. But what was worse, I could see it feeding on him—suckling on the side of his neck like a giant leech.

His eyes met mine, and for a moment his expression changed as a single tear fell from the corner of his eye.

"Help me, oh my lord, please help me," he plaintively begged, but as I watched, his eyes changed. They became grey, glassy, soulless, like gazing into the eyes of a shark.

Before I could even contemplate an action, let alone move, his visage shifted into the foulest contorted grimace imaginable. A cold shiver ran down my back as an inhuman voice expelled from the vicar's mouth, cursing me in a cruel and vile tongue before he was on me. In answer, I endeavoured to bring out my pistol, but he advanced with such ferocity I never had a chance to get a shot off.

One of his sweaty hands seized my wrist where the pistol was held, while the other wrapped around my neck and squeezed as he drove me backwards, tumbling onto the floor.

I recall my head hitting the ground. Hard.

I believe I may have lost consciousness for a brief moment, as when I opened my eyes, I was greeted by a slathering lunatic looming over me, saliva dripping from his bottom lip while he did his best to throttle me. There was a coolness from the back of my skull, which I rightly diagnosed as a head wound from whence I had hit the ground, yet fortuitously due to the sizable dose of drugs I had taken earlier I felt next to no pain.

My feeble attempts to break free turned out to be to no avail, as he gripped me with the strength of a madman, fingers digging into my throat. Finally, he thumped my right hand on the floor with such force as I was compelled to drop the pistol—seemingly my last hope gone.

Now, with the pistol lost, he moved in for the kill, using both hands to strangle me, trying his darndest to crush my larynx with his thumbs. I had one last hope and play-acted to be dying while rummaging through my pocket and retrieving my blue mistress: the hypodermic needle.

As my eyes bulged and I felt the world slipping away, I summoned my remaining strength, and with one final stroke plunged the needle into the neck of the mad vicar, depressing the plunger. I'd hoped to impale whatever the hell that was moving below his neckline, and it appeared that I must have been successful as the man immediately arrested his attempted homicide. He began to twist and thrash, spin and spasm, frantically trying to extract the syringe as he was engulfed in a drug-fuelled seizure. Finally, after what seemed an eternity but was probably chance nay more than a minute, it all stopped, and he moved no more.

There I lay in a bed of bloodstained bread, choking, straining to get air while my heart raced.

And then I heard the sliding noise from the blackness, the same noise I had heard in the dispensary, at first faint, and then louder...

Frantically I sat up and felt around in the darkness, despairingly trying to locate the pistol—when above me I heard it. I raised my head warily, and there, looming above me from the deck beam, was an undulating slick, jet-black shape from the pits of hades. A serpentine form, but in the place of a head, a maw filled with row upon row of jagged teeth, and the tormented shriek it made almost drove me insane on the spot.

It's somewhat farcical when your life flashes before you. Time quite literally slows down, despite the fact that you are paralysed with fear while damnation is relentlessly descending towards you.

It was two years ago, and I was with my Heather and the boys on a riverboat. We were on a summer holiday in the Cotswolds and were headed to Bath to visit a cousin of hers. The sun was out, shining on fields of green, and there was the smell of lavender on the wind. Heather smiled at me, and I smiled back. It was the first genuine smile I had made since her passing.

"*I'll be with you soon, dearest,*" I said.

But she just mournfully shook her head and replied without moving her lips, "*It's too late for that, my beloved.*"

Above me the eldritch horror descended, maw quivering in anticipation, when out of nowhere a silhouette in the darkness moved and a fist snapped out, catching the funnel-sucking nightmare in mid-flight.

All I could do was sit there as they proceeded to brutally whip and wallop the serpent on the ground repeatedly, as the abomination shrieked in torment. I

65

did my best not to retch as I heard a sickening splat noise—and the smell, oh god, the smell.

The shadow paused for a moment to inspect the parasite before a final slap, this time a horizontal swing onto a shelf, and the worm exploded, sending black ichor flying about the room.

Including a couple of droplets hitting me in the face.

I didn't move an inch as they tossed what was left into the darkness, turned, and moved ominously towards me.

"Get up off your bum. We've got to get off this ship now," ordered Lucy.

The vicar…Samuel … was dead.

There I stood over him, in total shock, looking down at the poor man in a pool of his own blood. Apparently he had bled out from the wound in his neck where that thing had been feeding on him.

This is all my fault, I self-remonstrated.

Lucy walked up beside me, looked down at the vicar, and as if she could read my mind, replied with a mischievous smirk.

"Well, looks like you went and got him killed, doesn't it?"

I turned in disbelief at the harshness of the statement, whereupon she snorted and continued.

"Look, stop being a damned dullard. They brought you down here to be fed to the hunger that resides in the main hold. They are bloody everywhere—it's just you and me now."

I swallowed the remaining moisture left in my mouth; now that I was made aware of it, I could literally feel the malignancy through the walls, the hatred, the malice.

Those … worms... were everywhere, and effectively everybody on board was either now under their full control, or consumed, no … subsumed by the devourer in the hold. I looked down at the vicar and at the wound on his neck. These blood suckers produced anticoagulants to stop clotting, so even if you could remove the parasite, you wouldn't be able to stop the bleeding.

Oh Lord, they are all doomed, they are already dead, walking cadavers, they just don't know it.

I took a deep breath, trying to summon the remaining stiff upper lip I had left, sifted through the bread, and located my revolver.

Quite simply, we either got off this boat now...or … well ... we never would.

The whaler boat was currently tethered behind the Varnae, so if we could get to it, we could slip away into the fog before they would notice us gone. From there it wouldn't matter; to be brutally honest, death by starvation or dehydration was by far preferable to the nightmare of the funnel-sucking worms.

As we headed towards the stairs, we moved briefly closer to the nightmare in the hold. The air was thick, and I felt my courage wavering as we climbed the stairs. Gripping the handrail, I physically pulled myself out of the pit.

I'd convinced Lucy that I needed some medications from my room. Of course, I didn't say what kind, but as I placed my hand on the doorknob, I heard sounds from within my cabin. My breathing ceased, and slowly, ever so slowly, I released my grip, trying to prevent the doorknob from creating a sound.

As I withdrew my hand, I breathed a sigh of relief. But of course, this meant I couldn't get to my medicine bag, and I would be coming off opiates while drifting in the ocean. Not exactly ideal, but it could not be helped.

Next, we swung by what I first thought was Lucy's room, but soon realised it was the darkened room the professor had entered.

"Wait out here," she instructed, and I did as she directed, of course.

I can't say I enjoyed standing there. I was still hallucinating, and every creak of the ship sounded like a moan or a wail. The hanging dividing sheets reminded me of the taxidermy skins I had seen earlier, stretched, and dripping blood. The line between dream and reality was well and truly gone, and I would now have to rely on Lucy. Not exactly a comforting thought.

It was only then that I thought I perhaps heard a struggle, but before I could enter the room, Lucy burst out of the blackness holding a tube.

"We need to go...now!" she insisted, and when I suggested that we grab some food from the pantry on the way, she replied, "We won't need to." From that, I took that she already had provisions, but I wondered where.

Up the stairs we went in haste, attempting to retrace the path poor Samuel and I had taken earlier, but in reverse.

Even though there was no one about on the berth deck, I could have sworn I heard quiet sobbing from the crew area.

Upon ascending the stairs to the gun deck, I glanced around for the Marine I had encountered earlier, but surprisingly he was not at his post. Scanning around I spied, at the other end of the ship, near the manger, a lantern on the ground and the silhouette of a figure lying on the floor. As my eyes came into focus, I noticed the figure seemed to be having a grand mal fit. Despite what was happening, my first reaction was to assist him, and I was about to head in his direction when I noticed shapes moving, writhing, under his uniform coat.

I don't know how long I stood there unable to breathe before Lucy grabbed my shoulder almost dragging me up the stairs.

Upon making it to the quarterdeck we were beset by the fog, which was now so heavy you literally couldn't see two feet in front of you. Out there in the murk, we could hear voices, but ominously I could neither identify the speakers nor indeed the language. Yet it was not the voices off in the gloom that concerned me.

Behind the stairs from whence we emerged was the ship's wheel, and there tied to it was Captain Baines, unconscious or dead, for it did not matter as blood dripped from an open wound on his forehead. What was most disturbing was that he had obviously been repetitively beating his own head into the wheel.

Despite the horrors, Miss Lucy seemed to be unaffected, and avoiding the lanterns in the gloom she led me through the fog to the larboard gangway, whereupon she started to descend the rope ladders while I stood there on guard. It would be a perilous swim, but I was an adequate swimmer, and as my assessments of Lucy had been woefully incorrect up till now, I thought it sensible to not wager against her athletic ability. So, as such, I was confident our plan had worked.

That was until I heard the booming Danish voice of Erasmus Järtlös.

"And where exactly would you be going in the dead of night, my dear?"

From out of the pitch darkness loomed the towering man.

Thinking quickly, I fabricated an embarrassing story of lovers slipping away where no one could see us and asked him to simply be a good man and look away.

He didn't believe a single word of it. In fact, he reacted as if I wasn't even there as he addressed Lucy directly.

"Lucretia—the game is over, and I believe you have something that belongs to me."

Lucy gave me a pensive look, which I immediately understood and responded by mouthing the words, "Go, I'll hold them off."

Pulling out my revolver, I trained it on Järtlös.

"Sir, I must insist you do not intercede in our leaving. Trust me, I have absolutely no compunction in taking you down."

If he was indeed frightened, he certainly didn't show it. To the contrary, in fact, his forehead creased, and he scowled with what looked like irritation.

"Yes… your final piece on the board. A brave knight attempting to save his bitch of a queen. I wonder if he'd be oh so gallant if he knew who you really were my dear?" And as he soliloquised, he nonchalantly released a single button on his greatcoat, allowing it to splay open.

My hand wavered from what I observed beneath that coat. Here there should have been a waistcoat or a shirt, or anything actually, but in its place was only blackness. Alike that room downstairs, it was a total absence of light that weighed on my soul. I found I couldn't stop staring, my gaze was transfixed, and I believe I began to see movement, shapes in fact, swimming in that nothingness. A movement that stared back with countless unseeing gazes.

It was all I could do not to fall to my knees and start screaming.

Before I could do anything, he issued a cold command, "Idiot, lower your damn arm and get the hell out of my way."

I cowered and meekly did as he spoke.

As God is my witness, I am not some good-for-nothing-cur. I've been yelled at by the best. By officers and drill sergeants, men trying to kill me and those I've killed. I honestly tried to shoot that arrogant bastard in his smug face, but it was as if Järtlös reached out with his words and ripped my remaining will to live right out of my chest.

Regardless, I dropped my arm and stepped aside.

To the night he announced, "Go down there and get me the map. If she resists, rip her bloody arms off and then drown her."

From said night emerged the two sailors he arrived with, only now misshapen beasts, ghoulish doppelgangers of the men I saw earlier. Their speech was alike animals cackling, and they had the smell of blood on their breath.

I gazed down at my limp arm and desperately tried to raise my pistol, but all I could feel was hopelessness. It was as if I could feel Järtlös's will holding my arm down.

In the back of my mind, I imagined Lucy's singing from before. My gaze happened to fall to my right, at the 32-pounder Carronade and its gunpowder cannisters. The canisters normally should not have been there; they were only brought up from the hull if the order to arms was given, but for some unknown reason the cannons were all ready to fire at a moment's notice.

This was a fatal error.

Fool was I, for this thing was not the girl I knew,

With dying breath, pulled out the knife, and slew it too.

My head turned and I looked at Lucy, jet black hair billowing in the wind while she hung there on the ropes just above the water line, and I gave her a forlorn smile.

Aiming at the canister I mouthed, 'Stalemate,' and pulled the trigger.

To be fair, it wasn't a hard shot, but I enjoy the irony that I hit it bang-on with my first round.

The initial detonation took out the gun emplacement and large sections of forecastle quarterdeck, including the section I was standing on, sending me hurtling into the freezing water. Unfortunately, or perhaps fortunately, considering the horrors on board, the blast created a cascading series of explosions, and without a crew to fight the fire, the entire ship was soon ablaze. The shrill screams of worms and the plaintiff cries of the crew echoed into the night.

As I have already said, I'm an average swimmer, but with the concussion and burns I soon dropped under the water. Thrashing, I made it to the surface for another breath but before long was below again. I mustered all my strength and broke the surface yet once more, beating the water for all my worth before falling under for a third and final time.

I awoke to the silent moon looking down at me, lying on my back with my head in Lucy's lap. We were on the whaler boat, the fog was now gone, the stars were out, and it would have been an enchanting view if not for the burning vessel filling the night sky. Even at this distance, I could feel the heat on my face from the fires on board.

Pain had returned, to confirm that I had been out for quite some time, and creeping into my mind was the terror of drug-fuelled hysteria, delirium, and hallucinations.

A most awful thought entered my mind.

I sat up and apprehensively turned to Lucy. Her eyes shone in the firelight as I asked, "Were there really monsters, or did I hallucinate it all and kill everyone on board?"

Lucy's deep red lips formed a wicked grin, and in response she purred, "Does it really matter, darling?"

She then kissed me with those cold lips.

A Dream of Blue and Green

Awoken from cryo-sleep, Yan and his fellow astronauts are tasked with assessing the alien world of Kepler 6020e for human habitation. Yet plagued with visions of the blue-green planet's destruction, Yan begins to wonder what's more important: finding a new home for humanity, or protecting the life already there?

About the author: W.A. Hamilton
W.A. Hamilton is a Canadian speculative fiction writer based in Halifax, Nova Scotia. His short fiction has been published in *Seize the Press* and *Daikaijuzine*. He is currently working on a debut novel. In his spare time, he enjoys board games, bouldering, and hiking. You can follow him on https://twitter.com/WAHamiltron or https://bsky.app/profile/wahamilton.bsky.social

Yan dreamt of Kepler 6020e each night. In low orbit, the lush, cloud-swept surface of the exoplanet was a constant out of the viewports of HOPE-60 station. Before settling his sleep mask into place, Yan would stare at the world below from the blinking semi-darkness of his pod, fingers tracing the glass like a mariner mapping distant continents.

Similar to Earth, yet unmistakably alien.

Stepping from the lander on their first mission to the surface, Yan remembered the explosion of foreign vegetation that had greeted the three astronauts: groves of slender fungi-like trees, stretching hundreds of feet into the misty air, while trailing tendrils gathered the moisture. Beneath the fungal groves, thistle-down moss and shifting carpets of hollow reeds; their stalks reaching to almost chest height on Yan's vacuum suit. And the colours — shades and tones that defied the imagination: iridescent purples and pastel pinks, fading to deepest blue and dusky orange.

Yan yearned for the sounds of it, the smell of it. He wanted to listen to the rustle of the wind in the alien trees, feel the texture of the leaves between his fingers. Instead, there was only the stale hiss of his own breath, echoing back through the suit's respiratory system.

As if reading his mind, Tosh tapped on the visor of her own helmet. "Don't be tempted to take these off. We can't be sure if the air is safe."

Yet Yan had been tempted. Sometimes he dreamt of removing his suit and wandering off into the jungle, the mossy tumble soft as down beneath his feet. Sometimes, in those dreams, he would find himself lying amidst a grove, staring up at the blue-green sky, and feel a sense of peace so deep all thought melted away.

The dreams were always like this, after trips to the surface of Kepler 6020e: buoying his faith in the mission. Perhaps it was the lingering effects of the cryo-sleep, but this planet felt *right* to Yan. Like it had been waiting for him. And with enough care and study, he was sure he'd find a way to map the delicate balance of Kepler 6020e's ecosystems, to understand how the planet's many forms of life fit together.

Visits to the surface were staggered a few weeks apart, giving Yan plenty of time to wrestle with such puzzles. As the days stretched between each visit, the mood aboard the station would become darker — perhaps the inherent claustrophobia of their situation, perhaps the isolation or the stress of the mission. Yan couldn't say for sure.

And Yan's dreams would shift to match. The blue-green sky of Kepler 6020e would rain ash, coating the surgical white of his vacuum suit. The delicate groves would go up in curtains of flame, reeds melting like wax paper while silhouettes of vast ships descended from the sooty clouds above.

Yan knew where those dreams came from; knew all too well the role he played in the world's eventual colonization. He tried to ignore the nightmares, to not read them as somehow prescient. He and the others would labour over their tests: analysing samples of soil, water, vegetation, even small organisms they'd captured — this world's flimsy version of insects. They hadn't found anything more evolved than dragonflies on the surface, even after extensive drone surveys. It was a young world, still hundreds of millions of years away from sentient life.

Yet every test confirmed their burgeoning hope — a hope that had seen Yan and his two companions flung hundreds of light years across the galaxy, suspended in cryo-sleep aboard their solar cutter; a hope for the future of the human race.

Could this world be a new Earth?

"Did you sleep well, Yan?"

The pleasantly melodic voice of HOPE-60's eponymous AI intruded on Yan's thoughts. Half-asleep, he'd been staring out the viewport at the surface of Kepler 6020e, spinning imperceptibly below them. Feeling a flicker of annoyance at the intrusion, Yan pulled aside the webbing that secured him to his sleeping platform and floated toward the hygiene station.

"Yes, I did. Thank you for asking Hope."

HOPE. *Habitable orbiting planetary exostation.*

"The others are already awake and eating in the kitchen," Hope informed him. "I'm glad you're up. I've compiled a list of priority tasks to complete in the next orbital period, which we'll review together when you join us."

Hanging weightless as he fumbled for his toothbrush, Yan nodded. "Okay, sounds good."

A brief click sounded over the nearby comm unit, Hope's way of letting him know she wasn't actively monitoring the conversation any longer. Yan rolled his eyes, glad the AI had limited visual sensors in the sleeping pods. There was no real privacy on the cramped station, but Hope's perpetual presence didn't make things any easier.

The AI's role was ostensibly to monitor mission priorities — more of a talking checklist than anything else — but she'd begun to feel more and more overbearing during the past months. Every morning, she woke the crew and set their tasks for the day, even reminding them to exercise and sleep at the appropriate times.

Hope had no real control over the station's onboard systems, so it was the humans who did all the actual work, but Yan was still forcefully reminded of his first lab manager, a tiny ham-fisted man who'd been unwilling to bend the rules even a fraction.

It did not take Yan long to change. When he reached the kitchen deck, the others were still eating. As always, he had to momentarily adjust as he entered the simulated low-g of the main deck. The central body of HOPE-60 was a rotating cylinder, containing the kitchen, main labs, and control deck. Gyroscopic motion provided the illusion of gravity for the crew, while various sleeping pods and lab stations split off like the branches of a many-limbed tree.

Tosh muttered a greeting, already skimming over the readouts from their last batch of tests. Ennita signed 'good morning' with her free hand, a half-consumed nutrient pack dangling from her lips.

Something had gone wrong with the cryo sequence for Ennita on their journey to Kepler 6020e.

She'd only half-slept, drifting in and out of moments of wakefulness; sometimes dreaming, sometimes horribly aware of the blackness around her. She'd woken from the de-hibernation process in a state of 'prolonged acute stress response', according to Hope, unable to form sounds or even understand where she was.

Yan could remember how she'd flailed to get away from him, brown eyes filled with an animal terror. Groggy with cryo-sleep himself, it had taken Yan the better part of an hour to soothe Ennita and persuade her to use one of the writing tablets to communicate with them. Yet even after the acute panic had passed, some primitive terror continued to lurk in Ennita's eyes; the indelible mark left by centuries with only the stars for company.

Once they'd settled into life aboard the station, Hope had begun to teach Ennita rudimentary sign language from her database, allowing her to resume basic mission functions. Nonetheless, Hope's lack of therapeutic programming had been a limiting factor in Ennita's recovery, one of many oversights on the part of mission control.

Despite this, Ennita was getting better. For weeks, she'd struggled with insomnia and taken sleeping pills, but the night they'd returned from their first mission to Kepler 6020e, she'd slept the whole cycle without assistance — greeting Yan at breakfast with a smile.

Time in nature was all I needed, she'd joked to him.

Now, it had been nearly two weeks since their last visit to the planet, and the cycle of sleep-insomnia was playing out as it usually did. Yan could see the dark circles under Ennita's eyes again.

Yan got his nutrient packet from the locker, but he'd no sooner taken his seat than Hope's cheerful voice sounded over the comm. "I have a mission update for everyone," she said. "Our priorities will be shifting, based on the parameters assigned to me at programme launch."

Tosh set aside her tablet. Yan and Ennita exchanged a look somewhere between dread and resignation. Hope's updates were rarely good, throwing the humans out of whatever routine they'd established and into the next phase without warning. Like when she'd set them doing spacewalks to assess station integrity, during their second week out of cryo-sleep.

"What's the update, Hope?" Tosh asked when the silence began to stretch.

It had taken Yan a while to figure Tosh out. The stocky aerospace engineer did not seem to really *want* to be here. Perpetually impatient to move onto the next phase, her focus was ahead: spend as little time on the planet as possible, complete the tests quickly, and get to whatever came *after*.

Yan wasn't precisely sure what 'after' was. The journey to Kepler 6020e had taken their solar cutter over a century travelling at close to light speeds. He could see the little ship from the kitchen viewports, vast solar sails folded like a parasol, as it sat docked to the wharf extending from HOPE-60 station. Theirs was one of dozens of similar craft to make the journey across the galaxy, to identical stations remotely established over the preceding centuries: a grand survey of Goldilocks zone near-Earth exoplanets, generations in planning; the next leap in human exploration.

Yet the cost for the surveyors? When Yan and Ennita and Tosh returned home, they would find a world lost to time: family and friends hundreds of years dead and gone, while they'd aged only a few, preserved by cryo-sleep and the effects of relativistic travel.

For Yan, the decision had been simple — there had been nothing left for him on Earth. No siblings. Parents and relatives already long dead. A pile of debt from several postgraduate degrees in biochemistry and astrobiology. And a burning desire to do *something* worthwhile with his life. Easy. So what was there for Tosh?

"I'm pleased to announce we have completed the requirements for the current phase of the mission," Hope told them, her cheerful tone giving no hint of whether this would be good or bad for the humans. "The outcome of our testing falls within acceptable parameters to move forward with alpha protocol."

"What does that entail?" Yan asked, gripping his nutrient pack. He'd never been clear on all the phases and protocols of the mission. That was Hope's job.

"The next phase of alpha protocol is the redeploy-and-report scenario, activated where conditions for successful human habitation fall within a high probability threshold. As I'm sure you're aware, the statistical chances of encountering this scenario are less than one-hundredth of a percentile—"

Ennita's hands began to move, signing something. Yan's brain kicked into gear.

"Wait, wait," he interjected, trying to untangle the AI's obtuse phrasing. "Are you saying 6020e will be able to support human life? You're saying that we've found it…"

"We cannot know for certain whether Kepler 6020e fully meets the requirements for human habitation without further testing," Hope corrected him. "However, current results fall with the conditions set out by mission control for further—"

But Yan wasn't listening anymore. He'd seized Ennita in a double-armed hug, sending their nutrient packets bouncing across the low-g deck. "I told you, all those months of testing — I knew there was something special."

Ennita gave him a tired smile.

"What does this mean for us, Hope?" Tosh asked, pulling them back to the moment. "What does the redeploy-and-report scenario require?"

Yan noted how the other woman was gripping the tabletop. He paused, turning over the words in his head. *Redeploy. Report.*

No, not that. We're not ready for that.

"The redeploy-and-report scenario involves a relaunch of the solar cutter and a fully-crewed return trip to Earth. We will transport samples from Kepler 6020e for additional testing and report on findings directly to mission control."

"You're sending us back?" Yan levered himself upright as if confronting the AI might help. But, of course, there was only the disembodied voice.

"That's correct, Dr Oblow. I am sending you all back to Earth."

"But you can't do that," Yan protested, gesturing. He could see the faint tremble of Ennita's shoulders. "You told us we would have more time to study the planet. Months. Years. We need to learn more. We need to understand the planet's ecology, figure out how humans can live here without harming the biosphere before we can even think about—"

"I am afraid the decision of how human habitation will be established on Kepler 6020e is not up to you, Dr Oblow," Hope informed him, infuriatingly detached. "I apologize for creating the wrong expectations, but in rare cases where the compatibility match falls within a high threshold, our protocol dictates an immediate suspension of testing, so settlement efforts can begin as soon as possible."

"Then we'll send the samples back and stay," Yan went on, hardly knowing what he was saying. "We'll stay and we'll do the testing ourselves. This is a special place, like nothing humans have seen before—"

"We're not staying," Tosh interrupted him.

"It will be two Earth-standard centuries before another vessel makes the journey to Kepler 6020e," Hope informed them. "While this station is designed to be self-sustaining, your continued presence here would be counterproductive. Re-settlement protocol will be determined by mission control, based on the data provided by the initial surveys. You may have an opportunity to re-apply and contribute to settlement planning efforts, contingent on the results of your performance evaluation."

Yan snorted, knowing how that request would land.

"We're not staying," Tosh pressed. "Whether it's a new Earth or not, we can't. Our contract stated a maximum of three years and then we had to ship home."

"So what?" Yan threw up his hands. "Who are they to tell us what to do? We came all the way here. We get to make our own choices."

Tosh glared across the table, eyes flitting between him and Ennita. "Look, I understand you're doing this to protect *her*, but she has to go back into cryo-sleep eventually. Either that or die out here."

"She can speak for herself," Yan retorted.

Ennita, who'd watched the exchange, signed a simple 'wait' and drew a tablet towards her. She wrote in silence for a minute, before turning the message to face them:

I don't care about cryo-sleep, I care about who this decision impacts.

When we were back home, it was easy to see this as an abstract exercise.

Now we are here, it is different. This planet is real. It's full of life. We need to honour that.

Our decision will have consequences — for the people back home and for this planet.

So our choice is important.

Tosh crossed her arms but did not reply.

Hope's voice interjected over the comm. "While I appreciate your concern, Dr Bhatt, the issue you're posing is irrelevant in the context of the established mission framework — as we've discussed before. Rather than projecting your personal feelings onto the situation, I would suggest you take comfort in the knowledge that these ethical dilemmas have already been rigorously debated. The best thing you can do is follow protocol and play your part in ensuring the future of the human race."

Ennita slumped back in her seat, seeming to almost fold in on herself. And Yan could feel a weighty darkness descending upon him, like the black clouds gathering over the skies of Kepler 6020e, carrying their load of ashy rain.

"How should we prepare for redeployment, Hope?" Tosh asked.

"Thank you for your cooperation, Dr. Innis. Today I will need you to complete a full backup of sample data to the servers aboard HOPE-60. Tomorrow, we'll begin to load all original samples onto the cutter and then initiate the start-up sequence of the cutter's reactor…"

Yan let the words wash over him, an empty babble of technical details. He stared instead at the silhouette of the folded solar sails out of the viewport, the pristine surface of Kepler 6020e spinning below.

Yan had grown up in a grey town on the coast of a grey sea. There were no fish in that sea. The sky was always grey and Yan's mother always had a cough, which kept her in bed. She passed away when Yan was only eight. But he remembered how she would take him down to the seashore on Sunday mornings.

"Our ancestors once sailed from here to discover new lands," she told him, as he hunted for stones to hurl into the surf. "One day, you'll do the same and leave all this behind."

As a child, Yan hadn't believed her. Why would he willingly venture into such a vast emptiness, leaving behind the familiarity of home? Now, he knew better. Sometimes the emptiness of the unknown was preferable to the emptiness of what you left behind.

When he'd gone to college, Yan had researched the disappearance of the fish, as one of his first projects. His grandfather had been a fisherman, although Yan had never known him, so he'd felt a certain connection to the question. The answer he'd discovered had been equal parts banal and depressing.

Everyone had known the acidity of the sea was killing the fish. It was caused by runoff from common chemicals, manufactured in refineries near the coast. But stopping chemical production and finding alternatives had been expensive and inconvenient, so no one had done anything — until the fish were already dead.

Yan decided not to ask Ennita to help him. He couldn't be sure what decision she would make. He only knew *he* had to do it.

He could not allow Kepler 6020e to become another grey sea, left in humanity's wake. So when the cycle's work was done, he lay on his sleeping pallet until the others drifted off. Then he floated down to the kitchen deck. Yet when he got there, the airlock to the wharf was already open.

"I know where you're going, Dr Oblow." Hope's voice sounded quietly behind him.

"Yeah, uh, I'm going to the cutter," Yan said, almost forgetting his prepared answer. "Just doing some pre-ignition checks. Couldn't sleep, so thought I would get a start on it."

"Of course." Hope paused as if she would rather say more. "I understand that change can be difficult. Please do what you need to ease your mind. However, be aware Dr Bhatt is already conducting engine tests on the ship. I would recommend consulting with her before beginning your own checks. She should be returning shortly."

Yan waited on the low-g bridge wharf. Some part of him was relieved; Ennita had made the same choice. He wondered if Hope knew what they were doing, but had decided not to speak up, understanding her impotence in the moment — the AI was not programmed for discipline, nor equipped to dole it out.

Yet when Ennita floated through the airlock, Yan felt his stomach churn with the spinning motion of the station. *What if we've made a mistake?* Some part of him still longed to see Earth, one last time. But he saw the blue-green silhouettes of Kepler 6020e behind her and felt the rightness of their decision, even in that moment.

Ennita did not look surprised to see him. Her lips creased into a smile and, as she drifted next to him, she took his hand, intertwining her fingers with his; an answer of its own.

It was not long before the first muffled explosion reverberated through the airlock. More blasts followed, but the fire burned itself out quickly in the cutter's sealed interior. Together, they stood on the wharf, watching as the flames devoured the ship.

"How could you fucking do it?" Tosh's sudden voice came from behind, filled with a rage Yan had never heard before. She must have been woken by the noises. The stocky engineer's eyes went to Ennita. "I wondered about him, but you…"

Tosh's eyes stared unseeing at the wreck of the solar cutter, venting atmosphere through its viewports. Although the frame of the craft remained intact, no human would fly it again.

"I would have alerted you, Dr Innis," Hope said over the comms, "but my core program directive instructs me to prevent violence onboard the station. Given the situation, I thought it best to allow events to play out and preserve the data collected by our team."

"Shut up, Hope," Tosh said, eyes never leaving the husk of the cutter.

For once, the AI had no reply.

The naked grief on Tosh's face covered Yan in a wave of guilt. "I'm sorry," he told her. "I know you wanted to go home. But we couldn't let them come. You know what they'll do."

Tosh's chin buckled. "I don't give a shit about them," she said, surprising Yan. "She's waiting for me back there. Stuck in cryo-sleep. I did this for her. A forgiveness of all debts — that's what they said, wasn't it? A fresh start. And she was so sick."

Ennita went to put a hand on Tosh's shoulder, but the other woman shrugged it away.

"You could've let *me* go, at least," Tosh spat.

"But then they would've known," Yan pleaded. "We wouldn't have had the time to study the planet: to gather the knowledge, to understand how to settle it carefully, without destroying the life that's already there."

"It doesn't matter." Tosh snorted. "They'll come eventually. To find out what happened to us. You're only delaying the inevitable."

But we will have the answers ready by then. Ennita's hands trembled as she signed the words. *When they return to find us, the solution will be waiting for them.*

"There's a cryo-chamber on the station," Yan put in. "You can wait for them if you want. Hope they send you back home."

Tosh blinked away her tears, nodding. "You can't control this, you know?" she said. "When they do come, you won't have any say in what they do."

Yan shrugged. "Maybe, but at least we'll have done the best we can. A lifetime to find a way to protect this world. One can only hope it will be enough."

93

Ennita took his hand again, squeezing their fingers together.

Yan loaded the landing with everything he thought they would need, and then Ennita added everything he'd forgotten. There was enough fuel for several dozen return trips, but Yan wanted to save it for transferring their research back to HOPE-60.

Before they left, he and Ennita helped Tosh settle into her cryo-pod. As the lid sealed over the stocky engineer, Tosh's expression held a curious tinge of envy, as if some part of her wished to see how their grand gambit would play out. Yet once in hibernation, a peace fell over the woman's face that Yan had never observed before.

"I hope she makes it back," he commented, once Tosh was down.

Whoever she left back on Earth, she must've been very special, Ennita observed.

They hadn't heard from their resident AI since the night of the fire aboard the cutter, but Yan stuck his head into the kitchen deck for one last farewell.

"Goodbye, Hope," he called through the empty corridors of the station. "Hope you don't get lonely." He winced at his own pun, but there was no reply.

Their final descent to Kepler 6020e went by in a daze. Dropping through the upper layers of cloud, the familiar blue-green landscape unfolded before them,

94

the trees and the lush underbrush getting larger and larger out of their viewports. At last, the final landing gear settled into place and Yan took Ennita's hand again, through the gloves of their vacsuits.

They stepped gingerly down the ladder, staring at the alien landscape of fungal trees and swaying reed stalks, the shades of their shared technicolour dream. Yan had run a series of tests over the last orbital period to answer his most pressing question — and determined the risks were low enough, at least for a few minutes.

"Shall we do it together?" he asked Ennita.

She nodded and, in unison, they popped the seals on their helmets.

A smell hit Yan's nostrils like nothing he'd ever experienced before. A spicy, peppery musk mixed with a deep sweetness — his olfactory receptors grappling with compounds they'd never been exposed to before. Yet the air, the scent of fresh, moisture-rich oxygen; that was the same. Yan closed his eyes and breathed deeply.

It would not be easy living here. In his head, he went through the mental checklist of the things they'd need to survive: edible plants, sources of freshwater, and materials that could be used for building or making tools. And for each step, they would have to test every scenario; taking every precaution to protect the fragile world around them; minimizing contact until they could study its impact. For now, the tiny landing craft would be their bed, kitchen, and lab. Yet one day — if something didn't kill them along the way — perhaps they could make a nest in these groves, string up a hammock and a tent of woven reeds to keep out the rain.

He turned to Ennita. Her face was tilted back to the blue-green sky, filled with a serenity that mirrored his own. Yan put an arm around her, pulling her close, and heard her sigh.

Abyssal Fire

When the royal warship the *Sky Queen* burns, Rhandras is brought before Duchess Blackthorn. He is commanded to investigate with the assistance of the Redcloaks, an order of warrior priests sworn to maintain human rule over Rhandras' kind.

About the author: Christopher McKinstry
Christoper's passion for writing has been reinvigorated by joining the North Shore Writers Group. He previously studied at Auckland University, graduating with a Bachelor of Arts in History (Hons). He lives in Auckland with his family and dog and always has a writing project on the go.

The blood moon carpeted the carnage in an eerie reddish light. A fierce wind desperately tried to deprive me of my cloak, while I equally desperately tried to hold onto it. Heat washed over my face as the timbers shrieked and roared, the hull twisting in on itself. It was a terrible way for a ship to go. Not at all an honourable death in battle.

Fire elementals danced among the ruins, spreading their burning gift. They were a noisome lot. Now, as I stood on the wharf, watching the flames devour the ship, I smiled.

The *Sky Queen* had once been a majestic ship. A warship, its sleek sides lined with closed gunports, sails furled about its masts. A powerful asset in the royal navy. No longer.

My mistress, Duchess Emma Blackthorn, was responsible for its protection. How would the king react to one of his ships burning under Duchess Blackthorn's watch? I suppressed the urge to laugh.

I would have to return to her, my position at her court allowing me to work against the humans under their notice. She might blame me, as an abyssal. She would need someone to present to the king to avoid her own punishment. That someone couldn't be me – I was her little abyssal, her pet, her useful servant. I could do things no human could, even with training.

I slipped into the crowd, pushing my way through, until I found an alley from which to further observe the unfolding destruction.

A throng of people formed at the docks, watching the great ship consumed. Many of the soldiers had to keep them from crowding too closely and endangering themselves and hindering the efforts to contain the blaze. Questions burned through them like the fire elementals would have.

"How did this happen? Who let an abyssal out?"

"These are Blackthorn's ships! She'll be furious."

"Forget Blackthorn. What will the king do?"

"What if it was the Breachers?"

"They're a myth. Or wasting their time. The breaches are sealed."

Long before I manifested, the breaches between realms sealed. My people, fleeing their failed invasion of this realm, were trapped, subjugated. I shuddered at the thought of my once proud people being reduced to serving humans. The Breachers worked to find a way to reopen the breaches. Not a group I associated with at all.

A figure in a red cloak appeared, a helmet covering its face. I suppressed the urge to run. One of a 'holy order' that occasionally gave their services to nobles. Always on their own terms. For their own reasons. Largely anti-abyssal reasons. And money. Lots and lots of money.

They made their way through the throng, the soldiers averting their gazes. When they reached the water, they held their arm out, produced a knife, and cut themselves. Three drops of blood fell into the water as they invoked the elementals.

They didn't speak pure abyssal, but a version the priests claimed to have cleansed for human tongues. It sounded like the shrieking of torn sails. Blue elementals rose from the water and began tangling with the fire elementals, while rain fell from above. It was too late, of course, with the *Sky Queen* already smothered and the wind frenzied.

I peeked above my cover with a dagger-thin smile. Their precious warship wasn't so intimidating now, was it? And the elementals had leapt to other ships by now so that a row of warships was on fire. The more, the better.

Duchess Blackthorn did not seem to suspect anything when I saw her, the next morning. After a sleep interrupted by dreams of the abyssal realm, the home I had never visited, ruled by my ancestors and rightful sovereigns the abyssal lords, I had my solitary breakfast. I was then summoned to her presence, as usual.

The red-cloaked soldiers, their faces concealed beneath visors as dictated by their 'holy' orders, took me to the conservatory at the rear of the palace. I was greeted with the sight of my duchess, holding her baby daughter, Sasha.

The garden was filled with plants from around the world, hedges arranged into neat rows and dotted with fountains. It was what humans considered lovely, and Blackthorn's pride. I wasn't allowed in, of course. Not that I found it at all beautiful.

When the soldiers announced my presence, Blackthorn looked up from cradling her child and smiled at me, the dawn's light playing across her face reminding me of the flames dancing across the ships.

"It's delightful when the morning sun catches the garden in full bloom, isn't it, abyssal?"

"I suppose, Ladyship."

With her long red locks, bright blue eyes, and the baby in her arms, Emma Blackthorn strived for the coarse human ideal of beauty. But the warmth in her eyes was fake, and her casual, friendly tone was too artificial. Unless I just couldn't appreciate the effect, as an abyssal.

I never would understand humans, nor did I want to.

"I have a job for you, Rhandras. The burning of the *Sky Queen* cannot go unanswered. Elementals were used, meaning either a rogue abyssal did it, or some human with training. They could be a danger to anyone." She gazed at Sasha for a long moment. "To my daughter. And until they are caught, the king will not trust me, at the least. You must find who did this and bring them to me so I may present them to the king." She rocked baby Sasha as she spoke.

"Yes, Ladyship." I hadn't expected that.

Duchess Blackthorn rocked Sasha.

"Rhandras, my dear abyssal, is going traitor-hunting for me. Isn't that exciting?" she cooed.

My stomach turned over. Was this a cruel joke of the abyssal lords?

Blackthorn continued. "Red-cloaks, you will accompany my abyssal. Rhandras, they will protect you, and watch you."

The red-cloaks stepped up beside me and nodded to her.

This was excellent. Sent to 'find' a culprit whose identity I knew very well and whose safety I was at least tangentially concerned about, accompanied by priests who were my people's sworn enemies.

After all, it was my blood that had summoned the fire elementals. If I survived this, I'd come back and burn down her precious garden.

The fact Blackthorn gave all these orders while cradling a baby and looking the epitome of nurture made it all the worse.

Horse and Norm

Horse and Norm have been friends forever and they finally
purchased their dream fishing boat. On their maiden
voyage they dredge up something dark from the lake.

About the author: Suzanne Bradley
Suzanne has been writing since like forever. She has a
master's degree in Screen Production focused on Script
Development. She also runs/plays tabletop RPGS.
Suzanne is currently rediscovering her passion for the
rhyming story. She lives in Auckland and has been with
the North Shore Writers group since its inception.

The sun was low and spirits high,
No cloud obscured the bright blue sky
The trees would sway as summer chills,
Their whispers heard beneath the hills.

Horse and Norm were by the lake,
A long-held dream was theirs to take,
Their jolly boat still on the shore
And time, they knew they wanted more.

Their childhood wish had been acquired
And just before the two retired,
For many years they'd scrimped and saved
For what they both had always craved.

Their calls and shouts the forest heard

And scaring every kind of bird,
Their flapping wings dislodged the leaves
That floated down on summer's breeze.

A bond had been forged in water and flame
A friendship and past that carried no name

There was a splash, the boat was out
And Norm, he gave a gleeful shout.
He waved to Horse still on the sand
And asked him if he'd like a hand,

But Horse, he stood with hands on knees
Breathing hard and with a wheeze
He raised a thumb, said all was good,
A few more tasks, then join he would.

Beside the road his Ute was parked
Within the lines so clearly marked.
The lake then drew his worried stare.
"I hope it's not too cold in there."

He then stepped out, his head held high,
The icy lake crawled up his thigh,
A mighty king from ancient halls
Until the water reached his balls.

Entwined in a dream had once been so bright
The passage of time would turn out the light

The day was spent with hooks and line,
Drinking beer and feeling fine.
Horse and Norm relived old days,
Of ocean shores in memory's haze.

Two quiet nights they'd planned to stay
Even if the sky turned grey
The catch was good and worth the wait,
They'd stay until they had no bait.

They counted fish, their haul admired,
The first star came, and they felt tired.
Horse went to lie upon his bed
His thoughts eclipsed with strangest dread.

Horse wasn't sure, but things were wrong,
And wondered if they'd stayed too long.
Into the night his dark thoughts spun
Until his sleepy brain was done.

The days that will follow are clearer than most
The vigilant man will not leave his post

When morning came, the lake was smooth
But Horse's thoughts it could not soothe.
They baited hooks and cast their lines
As wind picked up between the pines.

Norm felt a fish tug at his rod.
He then gave Horse a knowing nod.

They reeled it in with skill and care
The fish they caught, it wasn't there.

The silver box was worn and old
The keyhole's where the hook took hold.
Horse stared long then laughed with glee,
"Drop your line and catch the key."

Norm pulled it in and held it tight
Fingers clutched with all his might.
The box unhooked and in his grasp
He tried to open up the clasp.

A courteous whisper before their demise
The shadows slip through as darkness will rise

The box it glinted and it gleamed
And it was more than what it seemed.
Patterned swirls of strange design
And such detail in every line.

Horse then saw his best friend change
From something safe to something strange.
A certain look, the way he'd move
But in a way Horse couldn't prove.

Norm then turned to Horse and smiled.
His eyes were bright, a little wild.
"I'll open this when we return.
For now, it's none of our concern."

The Norm he knew was baiting hooks
But flicked the box strange hungry looks.
Something itched in Horse's brain.
He struggled with his thoughts again.

The fates had been waiting, for something to bind
On a dark shadowed shore the stars had aligned

Overhead the clouds had rolled.
It started raining, light and cold.
The wind was blowing through the trees
And Horse and Norm were ill at ease.

Their bucket filled with many fish,
It showed that they'd fulfilled their wish.
A day's success then moved to night
As two men drank their Amstel light.

There was no talk, no memory lane,
And all attempts were made in vain
As Norman's gaze was getting mired
In the silver box desired.

Horse's throat he tried to clear
And got up off his derriere.
"I think it's time we went to bed,
If I stay up, tomorrow's dead."

A horror had come from down in the deep

And into their hearts it had started to creep

Norm hummed and ha'ed with all his might.
He questioned if his friend was right.
With heavy feet Horse held his ground
And Norm stood up without a sound.

The boat was still it didn't rock,
And all his thoughts he'd try to block
But something still scratched at his mind
And left all sane thoughts far behind.

The morning came and all was good
Felt better than Horse thought it should.
But questions could be held at bay
So they could fish another day.

It was near noon, the sun was high
And time to leave for somewhere dry.
They packed their boat and headed home
Before the light began to gloam.

All mountains crumble and are swallowed as stone
And earth will endure, outlast flesh and bone

When Horse parked up and let Norm out
He spoke his question in a shout.
"You'll tell me what you find in there?"
What Norm had said Horse could not hear.

The nights were cold, a week passed by.
Horse heard no word, but had to try.
He called up Norm who answered quick,
His voice had sounded stuffed and thick.

"I've caught a cold," Norm said and frowned.
"I feel like I have gone and drowned,
I'm not quite sure I'll be okay.
The box was empty by the way."

Though not relieved, Horse wished him well
And offered to stop by a spell.
But Norm's response was cold and swift
And Horse had felt their friendship shift.

One man who is blinded by what he can't see
And there's nowhere to turn, and nowhere to flee

"You cannot help, I'm rather sick."
The phone cut off, an angry click
And Horse had felt his blood run cold,
But he'd not do as he was told.

He packed a lunch, a case of beers
And went to face his darkest fears.
A man like him won't leave his friend
He'd fight until the bitter end.

So off he drove to Norm's small house,
The one he shared with Jill, his spouse.

There was no sound, no windows cracked.
He called Norm's name, his nerves now wracked.

For moments there was not a sound,
No sign of movement could be found.
The silence scared him more and more
But still he walked up to the door.

A lingering shadow writhes beneath mortal skin
And causing a rot and decay from within

He steeled himself and then he knocked
And tested if the door was locked.
He strained his ears and closed his eyes
And prepped his mind for this surprise.

The things he heard from deep within
Had set his guts to cycle spin.
It was no voice he'd recognise,
It sounded just like swarming flies.

The door it creaked and then it cracked.
Horse raised his hands as if attacked.
The face between the frame and door,
It was not Norm, not anymore.

His eyes were grey and sunken deep,
Seemed like he'd been short on sleep.
His skin was red and badly scratched,
It looked like from him bugs had hatched.

As fingers and nails run ragged on flesh
Blood spurts from old wounds now opened afresh

Horse recoiled, and caught his breath,
It stank like Norm had messed with death.
Horse stumbled back, his eyes went wide,
Could not find words if he had tried.

Norm clutched the door so firm in place,
His body hid, showed half his face.
Out came his words bitter and broke.
What ghastly hell had Norm awoke?

Norm's three front teeth then tumbled out,
More boils before his eyes did sprout.
"Jill isn't well, does not look great,
I think I left things far too late."

Horse shook his head, looked to the street,
Finding strength to move his feet.
Norm reached a hand, said, "All is well."
But to his fear, three fingers fell.

What could be foreseen has now been obscured
No answer to prayers as the shadows endured

Tripping on cracks and chips in stone,
Ambulance called from mobile phone,
Into his Ute he struggled in vain

And dropped his keys into the drain.

Sirens were heard and Horse remained.
EMT's eyes silently strained.
Covered up, completed tasks,
Disgust behind their fabric masks.

No one spoke as bodies taken,
Just a wave that left him shaken.
A broken heart, his friend now dead,
Horse had no time, no tears to shed.

There was a task still incomplete,
And out of fear he might retreat,
The silver box he'd have to take
And cast it back into the lake.

Down to the dark where the light cannot touch
It seems like a lot, but it wasn't that much

Funerals came, the world was bleak,
Then off to Norm's one day that week.
What he had held he could not bear
 Now that his friend would not be there.

When he went back, the house was cold,
The food was off and caked with mould.
What he had thought should be undone
If he had known, he would have run.

He went inside and looked around.
With great relief, the box was found.
The bagged-up box against his hip
And it would take its final trip.

Horse, in his Ute, looked to his left.
Norman was gone, he was bereft.
Behind, the boat was towed along
'Cause keeping it felt very wrong.

He soon arrived down at the lake
And felt like it was no mistake.
He placed the box on Norman's chair
And with it left his pain, despair.

The flames rose high upon the deck.
He must be sure, he had to check.
It was a shock when jumping in,
The water cold on bones and skin.

Off the boat and onto the shore
He'd watch until there was no more.
The water kept the fire tamed,
The boat and box were now reclaimed.

Horse, he cried and wiped his eyes.
Stood on the wharf, flames on the rise.
And as night fell and cloaked the land
He felt an itch upon his hand.

No Fury

Eve, a woman scorned, gets revenge on her cheating husband, with fiery consequences.

About the author: Sharron Martin
Irish born New Zealander, Sharron Martin lives with her husband and three children in Auckland. Sharron spent most of her life working in the IT Industry and has published many technology articles and blogs, but always dreamt of becoming a 'proper' writer. *'Discovering Orla'* is her first fiction novel.
https://www.sharronmartinauthor.com/
https://www.goodreads.com/book/show/197412826-discovering-orla

"Sorry, what did you say?" Eve looked blankly at Tom, her husband of fifteen years. She thought he had said something about leaving her, but obviously that couldn't be right. He stared at her; brows wrinkled.

"I said, I'm leaving you."

The room tilted. Nausea pooled in her stomach and rose into her throat. Acrid bile leaked into her mouth; she swallowed it down. She put out her hand, reaching for something to steady herself.

"Oh, for goodness' sake, spare me the dramatics," Tom said. Reaching out he gripped her shoulders and pushed her down on to the sofa. Her heartbeat pulsed loud in her ears, and she struggled to compose herself. She looked out through the expansive glass doors of the holiday home they had bought together a few years ago. The dreamhouse on the cliff with panoramic ocean views and wrap around decks. They were so proud of its entertainer's kitchen, five bedrooms, two lounges and separate media room. The house that was supposed to bring their family together but had become nothing more than a source of bitter conflict ever since. Sunlight bounced off the mirror sea and blades of light pierced her eyes. She turned away and put her face in her hands.

"Oh, come on Eve. This can't be a shock. Not if you're honest with yourself. It hasn't been working for some time. You know that."

Did she? Did she know that? Things hadn't been great between them, that was true, but just lately things had been a lot better. They had not been fighting at all, and talking and laughing like they used to, and he had been so much happier. Tom sat across from her, glaring. She glared right back, noticing for the first time the new shirt, the stylish haircut and something else different that she couldn't quite identify. Had he lost weight? Fear twisted in her gut; an ugly realisation dawned. And then he said it.

"I've met someone else."

Months passed in a blur of appointments with lawyers, uncomfortable conversations, and discussions about who was entitled to what. At least the kids were in their late teens, almost adults themselves now, old enough to understand

116

apparently. Not that she did. Apart from a few questions about where they were going to stay when they came home from university, they seemed remarkably unflustered by the whole situation. There were even a few comments about how pleased they were to see their dad so happy. Well, I'm not bloody happy, Eve wanted to scream. It was truly shocking how quickly the life they had spent all those years building was torn asunder. Rendered meaningless, in no time at all, with a flick of a bright blonde ponytail.

"You've agreed to what?" her friend Olivia said, staring at her wide-eyed over her cappuccino as they caught up in Starbucks. "You've given him the beach house and the boat?"

"I don't want it," Eve replied. "I never really liked that house and what am I supposed to do with a boat?"

"Make him sell it, that's what. At least you'd get half the money," she said. "You're on your own now, starting all over again. You're going to need every penny you can get."

"I thought about it, Olivia, but if I do that then the kids miss out."

Olivia snorted into her coffee.

"I'm sure they'll cope, Eve. You do realise that if you do this, then she ends up with half of everything. You can't possibly agree to it. You need to go back to the lawyer; say you made a mistake. Temporary insanity, something!"

"It's too late, it's done. I'll just have to think of something else."

An expanse of petrol blue ocean greeted Eve the day she arrived at the beach house to collect her belongings. Her hand brushed against the feathered lace of the toetoe fronds that framed the driveway, statue-still in the warm, quiet morning. Bright sunlight cast silver ripples on the ocean as she made her way to the front door. Eve hesitated, beads of sweat mushroomed across her back and she felt her pulse quicken. As she raised her hand to knock on the door it burst open and out rushed a young woman wearing a tight white singlet that struggled to contain her oversized breasts and ridiculously high denim cut offs.

"Oh hi, you must be Eve, I'm Georgia. I'm so pleased to meet you. Tom told me how fabulous you've been about everything," she gushed.

Tom came out behind her, extending a protective arm around her tanned shoulders.

Smiling he said, "Yes, you've been incredible. Agreeing to let us have this house and the boat as part of the settlement, it's so generous of you, Eve."

Eve smiled back, trying not to stare at Georgia's tiny waist and impossibly long sun-kissed legs. She couldn't be much older than their own daughter.

"Come on in," Tom waved her through, as if it wasn't her own house, which of course it wasn't, not anymore. "I've made a start on a few boxes for you, but I know you'll want to go through things yourself.

We'll leave you to it, we're off out in the boat for a few hours so you'll have the place to yourself. You just take whatever you want, OK?"

"Yes, absolutely, whatever you want," Georgia repeated. "We're going out on the water. Tom's been teaching me all about it. I am just loving having a boat. Thanks again for that, Eve." She stepped in closer to her, blue eyes wide in her unlined child's face and said, "Oh, and just one thing, as the children's mother, I sincerely hope that we can be friends and parent them together. I think it's so important that everyone gets on, don't you?"

"Indeed, I do," Eve replied, flicking her gaze to Tom, who at least had the grace to look embarrassed by the comment.

"Come on then, let's give her some space," he said, ushering Georgia out the door and down the path to the jetty.

Eve watched them from the deck, happily chatting and laughing as they walked along in the sunshine. Weighed down with a picnic basket and beach bags filled with brightly coloured towels, everything they might need for a lovely day out on the water. Not a care in the world.

Once they reached the boat and started to load it up, Eve headed for the path. She held back and watched as Tom untied the rope and started the motor. Sitting at the helm he manoeuvred the boat slowly out to sea. Georgia sat beside him, sunglasses

119

on, laughing at some no doubt asinine comment or other.

After a furtive scan of the beach to make sure no one else was around, Eve felt for the remote control in her pocket. She blew a last kiss at her dear husband Tom, and firmly squeezed the button. The force of the explosion almost knocked her off her feet and blew the boat to pieces, shedding flaming detritus into the water. Angry red orange flames hungrily devoured what was left of the small craft. As she stood on the jetty watching the boat burn, she thought to herself that it was a bit of a shame, she was a pretty little thing.

Weavers' Curiosities

Weaver Brothers: curators; purveyors of practical magic; immortal

Thomas Weaver makes a bargain with a *witya* requiring close contact with the *hunten* – the brotherhood who slaughter the *witya* for power. Caught between two forces, Weaver discovers deeper mysteries at work, and learns not all deals can be undone without consequences.

About the author: Sarah Anderson

Sarah joined the North Shore Writers Group in search of guidance and inspiration in finishing her first novel – a project which lagged for years until she joined the group. When she's not writing, Sarah works as a lawyer where she uses words to create a different type of magic. She is currently working on a novel-length project where the Weaver brothers feature again.

Twenty years of routine covered the furniture of my life like dust - thick and dull and muted. The pages of my life's book turned slowly, and always I longed for another story.

Gideon would sweep in and out of our shop, an eddy of activity, pulling in the bustling of the outside world as though it mattered, a light kindling in his eyes as he looked beyond the window. We had become more different still, since all this began.

Lavinia was the breeze.

On that day, I had sat at the counter for hours, tracing the likeness of a birch tree from the vaulted window at the top of the tower room. The door to the curiosities shop nudged open, getting stuck as it always did whenever someone for whom the shop was not designed stumbled in. The fresh air carried the delicate scent of lotus flowers, and I let the graphite fall from my smudged fingers as the scent stirred me.

She had a pretty, open face and her eyes travelled on every impulse - behind her and above her, attention catching on the shelves and the artefacts Gideon and I had assembled. From her demeanour, I surmised she was used to going where she pleased, and from the quality of her dress, that she had coin to spare. Her eyes were a honey brown, and a smattering of freckles constellated across the bridge of her nose to rounded pink cheeks on either side. When she smiled at me, I stood, remembering a fleeting something long forgotten.

"Good morning, madam." I dipped my head as she approached. "What brings you to Weavers' Curiosities?"

"Before I entered," her voice was light but her tone was heavy, "I did not know." Her smile became at once familiar.

I offered her tea and showed her some of the mundane trinkets we plied - charms for restfulness, a mirror that revealed the most flattering features, and an assortment of candles that engendered an indefinable sense of comfort in the observer. We often sold these wares at the river market when times were tough and the risk of attention from the *hunten* was low. As we spoke, she confirmed she was the daughter of a nobleman. She did not know what I knew about the shop and its nature, and so she found it 'curious' that she had entered alone and without cause.

Weavers' Curiosities pre-dated our encounter with Ismay, but these days it was kept in the black by a unique offering to those who could find us.

There had been visitors over the years who had accidentally entered, those who did not possess the *summonata*, or sometimes, those who did not know that they did. But even very mundane yearnings will manifest in something more sometimes, and a desperate soul will be drawn on, as though by a cord about their waist, to the place they need to be.

Not being a *witya*, there was every chance that once Lavinia closed the stained-glass door behind her, she would forget her excursion save for vaporous memory.

But Lavinia returned every week for another candle, and then every other day. I began to wonder whether it wasn't *I* who was willing her to return, but Gideon and I had discovered early on we were unable to hold the *summonata* for long, and not without direct contact to a *witya*.

I did not believe that love was a force of magic until then. It had always been straightforward and strong by layers of effort. My father had loved my mother, my mother had loved her home and her

123

family. As we were born, we reinforced that bond, which was powerful, but still mundane.

In Lavinia, my world was struck with animation, such that I was bewildered by joy; overcome with a need to resume connection with the world once more.

In those months, my *re-awakening* as I would later think of it, my hunger for a remedy to my situation re-ignited.

It had been eighty years since we received our 'blessing' from Ismay, and since then we had not aged. It became a curse as our mother died, leaving our grieving, ageless father; as our sisters neared the end of their child-bearing days, and we had to leave town to avoid suspicion of *wityacraft*. When we were the image of our own great-nephews, our visits became infrequent and then too dangerous to continue.

When Ismay passed on, we felt it in our bones and wondered if our blessing was done. That had been twenty years ago.

Gideon was pleased with my 'resurrection' as he called it, but his brow furrowed when I suggested a union with Lavinia.

"How, Thomas?"

I looked away.

"If we were further away from Ismay's bloodline, it might weaken."

"We don't know. It might result in instant death."

Another option we hadn't yet tried. Our minor ailments and abrasions healed with unnatural rapidity. It would be years before we tried more drastic measures and found them equally useless.

The discussion became moot. Lavinia returned, tears in her honey eyes and a leaden weight she placed in my heart with the trembling touch of her gloved hand. She was betrothed.

The wind outside was unusually blustery. It whistled through the gaps in the window panes, next to where I had sat for the last hour, minding the shop from my reading chair in the corner. The wooden chime over the door knocked me out of my place on the page. The visit was not accidental.

I placed the book on the side table, and listened as a slow but steady meter of steps brought the tall, auburn-haired woman into view. Magisend's skin was unnaturally luminescent.

"The youngest Weaver."

I rose slowly.

"Mrs Drake." I returned her superficial smile and stood behind the counter, moving aside the graphite.

"I've come with a delicate task."

This gave nothing away, so I waited as she surveyed the artefacts on the nearby shelves. She picked up a candle, arching an eyebrow.

"You are uniquely qualified for this task, but I fear you won't like it."

"In that case, I fear you will not like the price."

She put the candle back and approached the counter.

"There is a particular *hunten* with something I need." She didn't elaborate.

"Are you looking for an intercessor?" Of course, she was not. The saving grace of being as we were, was the side effect of being all but invisible to the *hunten,* not that we had ever heard of them before Ismay.

"No. A thief."

"To take what?"

"Blood."

I turned back to my reading chair.

"I'm afraid there is no price high enough. We cannot attempt to kill a *hunten*."

"I don't need all of it, just a drop."

"Why?"

"I prefer not to say."

I tossed my eyebrows to my hairline and sat down. Outside, a large carriage blocked the view of the trees. It was similar to Lavinia's.

"Is there nothing that would make it worth the risk?" There was something hidden in her words. I decided to wait rather than chase it out. Magisend sat on the arm of the sofa across from me.

"I know that a certain duke's daughter visits here often. I assume she's not here for the candles she

126

buys."

"Threats will not warm me to your cause."

"Oh no, Mr Weaver. In exchange, I offer a solution to your problem. A talisman to allow a suspended man to age and die with his love."

Gideon didn't speak after I told him. He closed his eyes and put his large palm across them.

"It's not possible."

I poured the tea I'd set to brew, making sure Gideon's had the first and most potent portion.

"Magisend is as powerful as Ismay was."

"And far less trustworthy."

"I thought you liked her?"

"I like her coin."

We drank in silence.

"How will you take blood from a *hunten* and live long enough to enjoy your new life?"

I'd thought of little else since Magisend left. All I needed was a drop of blood, collected on clean cloth.

"What does she need it for?" Gideon sat forward suddenly, putting his tea down.

"It's not our business to ask."

Gideon's eyes were cold and still.

"If Magisend is using the same blood-craft as the *hunten*, it makes her no better than them."

Gideon rarely concerned himself with morality.

"Why are you against this? We've done dangerous things before. Don't you want a normal life at some point?"

He crossed his legs and sat back again, looking out the window to the pub across the street. "I like this life."

"You haven't always."

His eyes flickered and he looked back at me.

"Thomas, we were created as pawns for the *witya*."

"That's not true."

"Isn't it, though?"

When the wooden chime above the door announced Lavinia, I should have noticed that the door didn't stick. She glided in and with a taut smile that failed to reach his eyes, Gideon swept just as fluidly out. Lavinia took his empty seat and I watched Gideon cross the street and enter the pub.

"I know I ought not to come any more."

Against propriety, I took her hand. A small, gloved bird nested in my palm.

"We could leave."

"Leave the shop?"

"Leave everything."

"But where would we go?"

"Far away. We could live as townsfolk. Lay low. Get married."

Her eyes darkened and she shook her head,

"They would never let us live. My betrothed is a powerful man. He would hunt me; I have no doubt.

128

It is too dangerous."

I could see her mind was set. I nodded, placing her hand back in her lap. After an instant, she placed it back on mine, her grip firm.

"We must leave by ship. A new continent."

Hope lifted my face to hers. Her kiss was as delicate as a blossom and I saw our future, free and enamoured with each other. Our children would stand above our graves and endure, and we would pass peacefully and naturally on. It was reckless, rightful abandon. There was nothing I would not do to make this dream for us.

"There is something I must do first."

The next day I booked us both passage to New Holland the following week.

I don't know the origin of the *hunten*; I don't know that anyone now living does. Before Ismay, we knew only rumours in the tavern or the market that *wityas* were dark, unnatural beings who could manipulate the world to their bidding. Our father had always dismissed this as superstition. He preferred to believe in a god to explain what he couldn't understand.

'witya' were occasionally captured by *witya* catchers and dark deeds alleged. Then those who were accused were put to death by the religious zealots, making it unlikely they were actually *witya*.

The *hunten* on the other hand, never stirred a whisper. Which may itself have been their doing.

Since our 'suspension' we were awakened to the knowledge that while *witya* could manipulate the natural world, most rarely drew attention to themselves, and carried out no more harm than most people, less even. The *hunten*, however, were corrupted by their *summonata* and used it to wield influence on the world in a way the *witya* never would. Coercion, murder, immortality all required *summonata* in excess of what one person can store. The answer was in blood - the taking of power from another by force. Even mundane blood has a life force, which when extinguished completely, can be captured. From a *witya*, taking power is easily done on a small scale – a drop of blood or a strand of hair imbibed into the body. Its effects are fleeting, however. The lasting transference comes from the consumption of organs post-death.

Whenever a body was found, drained of blood or sans organs, we were reminded of the lurking danger.

We had always been an enterprising family, but armed with awareness of *wityas*, we carved out a unique market for such clients. The store flourished. Word spread, and we bartered discrete services for artefacts and items with abilities, as often as we traded for coin. Sometimes the artefacts were years in the making, but we had time to wait.

After only a few years, we had a silver throwing

knife that would never miss its target; an immortal plant with leaves that engendered calm and perception; and a plain brown cap, that made the wearer at once forgettable.

The hat was useful when a *witya* wanted to remain unseen; when evading the *witya* catchers or worse, the *hunten*. It came to us as payment. Though we had no need of its powers ourselves, being unseen by the *hunten*, we knew it *would* fetch a good price. It sat inconspicuously on a hook in the shop, together with an umbrella, which had no discernible qualities other than being waterproof.

If it allowed a person to be unseen; I wondered if the hat would allow me to be seen. I could be visible and at once invisible to the *hunten.* There would be no easy way to engage a *hunten* for long enough to obtain blood otherwise, short of brawling with one on the street - but we were only unseen by the *hunten*, and the last thing I needed was to find myself in a jail cell.

The one she wanted blood from was Lord Camrys. A noble whose villages paid taxes, but never too much, and whose servants were well paid. It was hard to believe he was a *hunten* except for the telltale signs of dark craft which marked him. Having too much *summonata* in a body compromised the facade it seemed, and the *hunten* presented with waxy, yellowed skin, sunken eyes, sores and other lesions which were slow to heal. Gideon and I often wondered whether our inability to wield the *summonata* partly explained why our bodies resisted decay.

Camrys maintained a permanent presence in the city, but it was well guarded and there was no easy way to gain entry.

It was Gideon who discovered that he also had a penchant for gambling.

"How did you find this out?"

Gideon's irritation was supreme.

"Would I let you do this alone?"

I had let it go. Gideon's vices were not a mystery to me, but it had been a long while since his nightly drinking and debauchery resulted in gambling. In the early days, there had been several debts I'd had to settle while Gideon, who had taken to his bed (with or without his consort of the night), did his valiant best to avoid the torture of waking life.

I shaved for the first time in years, resembling Gideon more by the minute. He preferred the convenience of a close shave; I preferred my anonymity. I tapped the blade on the stone basin before dropping it into the dish by the looking glass. Gideon handed me a towel as he pushed off the wall and peered out the window onto the street below.

"I've told you all there is to know."

"I need to see him."

"Have you got a plan?"

"Enough of one."

He paused at the door.

"Your tickets to New Holland arrived today."

The den below the public house was lit by low-hanging candelabras. Smoke created a screen through which incorporeal voices and gravelly laughter permeated in bursts. I moved around the room, peering through the gloom at corner tables and booths where gentlemen sat in various states of euphoria, induced by some substance or the presence of a forbidden companion. As I slipped the hat deftly onto my head, the returning glances slid out of focus, and the piano in the background dulled. I was unravelled out of memory as soon as I occupied it. There was evidence of someone: a chair occupied, an arm nudged, a drink consumed; but of the man who sat and nudged and drank, there were no discernible qualities.

The *hunten* sat straight-backed, frowning at his cards, his golden-red hair falling gracefully across his eyes. With his long, wax-white fingers, he deftly tossed two blue stones to land with a precise click, as though placed, in the centre of the table. Then he looked at me, eyes narrowing.

I wish I could say I nodded and walked by smoothly, having the sense to remove the hat as I did.

There is an innate awareness within living creatures that raises the hackles, quickens the breath, that springs the limbs in the ultimate pursuit of life's purpose - to continue. Humans are the only ones that

133

ignore it, pulling back just as blindly and walking towards death itself or, in my case, sitting at the card table next to it.

"We have not met.'"

"No, sir." I observed the dealer turning the cards over, as though he had not noted my presence in the small circle.

"Deal another hand." The *hunten* frowned as the dealer failed to place cards in front of me until the *hunten* intervened. He eyed me after a moment.

"You are unseen to them."

Ignoring the survival instinct, I leaned closer.

"All that matters is I am visible to you."

"Who are you?"

I glanced at my cards, unaware of the rules.

When Ismay gave us the gift, she had been hiding from a *hunten* whose name I invoked then, heart beating in my throat, clutching the knife in my pocket.

"A friend of Leocadius."

The *hunten's* face cleared.

"Leocadia?"

I didn't correct him. Wondering whether I had fallen on good fortune or frighteningly out of depth.

"Sir - how do you bid?" the dealer asked, looking through me.

Camrys looked back at his cards, irritated, and then tossed another blue stone which skittered across the circle, knocking another one out. In that instant of distraction, I removed the hat, watching as Camrys

134

turned back to me. I held his eye calmly, wondering whether I had, in bringing myself to his attention, lost my protection forever. But after a moment, a sharpness in the depth of his grey eyes dulled and his jaw dipped back to his cards.

I stood from the table. Several confused faces followed the movement, which was rather inconvenient.

The knife was sharp, and as I moved around the *hunten*, the barest knick of steel caught his neck.

"Terribly sorry, sir," I murmured, pressing a handkerchief to the cut immediately and retreating into the crowd as, teeth bared, his sharp eyes fixed on me and then drifted into vacancy. He touched his neck and I faded into the smoke.

I wiped the blade on the kerchief and tucked it into my pocket, barely breathing for how hard I was shaking. By chance I looked up at the balcony, scanning for watching eyes, and saw Gideon. He turned away after a solemn moment and re-joined the well-dressed young man next to him.

I left the public house, leaving the hat off for good measure and crossing the street. Standing beneath an oil lamp I observed the handkerchief, wondering if there was anything different about a *hunten's* blood.

I needn't have bothered.

The handkerchief was clean.

It was fortunate that Magisend stopped by the next day, as I'd barely ventured further than the cover of the few books on *summonata* we'd held.

I knew I'd mistaken the faint lotus scent that often preceded Lavinia when the book snapped closed.

"Mr Weaver. I didn't expect to find you here, sitting idly."

"Then why did you come here?"

She sat in my reading chair without being offered.

"He doesn't bleed."

I told her about the knife and the handkerchief.

"But you saw his blood?"

"I did."

"Was it on the blade?"

I couldn't recall. I'd not seen the knife, as it was dark.

Magisend sat folded over, eyes vague in this world as she considered something within her.

"I wonder. A tincture. If he would imbibe it…," she looked back at me. "Mr Weaver, it's time for you to come to *my* shop. Tomorrow. I'll have what you need. You must have him drink it though."

I would need a plan.

I waited outside the gambling den, in the

136

shadow of a nearby alley, the hat tucked into my pocket. Camrys slid down from an ornate, slick carriage the colour of tar. Unnatural. As was the way he walked, gliding smoothly down the stairs, back taut and eyes fixated.

Having discerned where he lived, I borrowed a plain-looking horse from an unattended carriage. It was easy, aided by the hat, and so much more efficient to manoeuvre one man atop one beast, than coagulate in the streets with the sluggish coaches. As I approached the gates to the stately house in the commercial district, I led the horse to the shadows and hoped it would remain unnoticed. I walked slowly but deliberately to the house, rang the bell, and breathed deeply.

I nodded to the doorman and slid past him inside, turning back as I crossed the entrance hall to see his brow furrow. He stepped outside, looking down the street.

I wandered through hallways, taking in the paintings on the walls. A tall, pale, flame-haired man was in many. Different women, different generations revealed by the changing style of painting. The resemblance of the Lord Camryses was unmistakable.

A chill plucked at my neck hairs.

Or unnatural.

The grey eyes in the face which should have been described as delicate, tracked me as I followed the voices of the servants.

It was the kitchen and the dining room that I

needed to see. The reason for the dalliance I didn't want to share with Gideon until after it was over.

There were three women in the kitchen kneading dough. Conversation was subdued and careful.

As I walked among them, I caught eyes that became distant; half expressions of surprise forgotten on slackening faces. I removed earthen bottles from shelves and peered inside. Oils or lard by the smell, seasoning, dried herbs. Nothing that would easily take a tincture or likely to be imbibed.

"I'll be pleased when this engagement feast is over," one of the women murmured. I paused and turned back.

"The master got additional servers for tomorrow. Besides, all you do is the basic stuff, it's us who work from dawn, flapping like hens-"

"-sweltering over pots-"

"-kneading till our arms fall off-"

"Where is the feast?" I asked quietly.

"In the main dining room of course," was the response after the arrested looks slid off three faces.

"When will the help arrive?"

This time the response was slower and the oldest woman had a wary look about her eyes that I didn't like.

"Midday. From Lord Carraway's household."

I slipped out of the kitchen and back through the house, stopping at the foot of a grand staircase. I had what I needed and it would be sensible to leave.

But curiosity was not cured by reason.

The largest painting halfway up the stairs was of a bearded man with thinning hair. His skin was wax-white, his eyes a deep blue. His robes marked him out as some kind of priest but I noticed he was floating above the ground. A saint then.

His features were not painted carefully enough, but there was a familiar tug at my memory. He resembled Gideon, or perhaps our father. At the same instant I registered the gilded placard below the painting, out the window the tar carriage pulled up to the house.

'Leocadia. The First.'

Camrys sprang out of the carriage, face contorted. The footmen backed away and I knew I had instants to make a choice before the door flung open.

Removing the hat, I retreated further up the stairs as the door burst open below. I crept into a side passage and saw salvation in the window at the end of the corridor. Beyond it, a flat-pitched roof I could climb onto.

"Bring warmed wine to my study," came the taut voice downstairs. Not knowing where the study was, I hurried to the window and was about to slide it open when a woman screamed to my right, holding blankets in front of her.

I put the hat on instantly.

"You imagined it," I murmured. The woman started and then dashed downstairs into the light.

"What was that?" he demanded.

"I'm sorry my lord, I thought I saw something. Only a shadow."

I pulled the hat off and immediately heaved the window open. It scraped loudly. I ignored it and vaulted over the sill, dropping onto the flat roof. I turned to close it and froze, arms raised.

Grey eyes narrowed in displeasure. I was close enough to see a vein in his temple, curling into red-golden hair.

For one held breath, I thought my immortality was ended. Then the *hunten* surveyed the window, running long white fingers over the frame.

"There has been an intruder." The chill statement was loaded with rage. I turned and ran, not daring to don the hat until I was far enough away to drop into a side street.

The hot breath on my neck buckled my knees. I turned to face the same plain horse I'd left earlier.

The dining room was covered in shadows, despite the feast commencing not long after noon. My damp palms were clasped behind my back in imitation of the other Carroway household servers, all standing paces behind the long tables arranged in rows. I stood behind the head table in my borrowed and ill-fitting Carroway tunic. Two empty seats at the centre awaited the *hunten* and his betrothed.

140

The tincture was heavy in the right pocket; the hat padded out the left. I'd considered not bringing it in case the *hunten* could see the hat when it was not worn. But it had been a lifeline to me, and I dared not leave it behind.

The windows were covered with sheer black fabric, distilling the daylight into a comfortable gloom. Outside in the distance I could see the roof of Magisend's townhouse. I'd always assumed she was pretending to be a noblewoman, but the brief venture to the stately house the evening before changed that.

She had led me through grand, light-filled rooms with impossibly high ceilings. Though there were no trees outside, green leaves branched their way in through tower windows. Mesmerised, I'd followed her to a small workshop with grey stone benches and plants of varieties I'd never seen. Then she had handed me the small green bottle which now sat in my pocket.

The doors to the dining hall clackered open and a carrying voice announced Lord Carys and his betrothed, Leofe of house Flanders.

Her form and her walk were so familiar to me by then that I didn't need to see the honey-coloured eyes for my heart to stutter. I cleared my throat, finding it hard to take in enough air as they sat in the vacant seats in front of me.

Lavinia had said her betrothed was a powerful man.

I pictured her married, immortalised in a

141

painting next to the others, while the real immortal endured.

I noticed a man dressed in a Carroway tunic eyeing me as he murmured to another. He nodded curtly and approached me, mouth set in a firm frown.

I pulled a small cloth from my pocket and, careful not to touch the surface that was damped with salve, I wound it around the pad of my thumb and pressed it against the man's arm as he drew near.

His frown relaxed as I reminded him I'd commenced service in Carroway's household just last week. He took the cloth from me and wordlessly walked away.

The *hunten* turned abruptly. His eyes tracked the man.

Lavinia's however, did not. Her mouth parted in an involuntary 'O' as she stared at me. At a cleared throat she hastily looked back at the *hunten*.

I lifted a carafe and poured first for Lavinia, noticing the fine blonde hair on her neck stand up. Circling behind her to the *hunten's* side, I was able to add the tincture to the jug as my back was to the room. The smell was potent and a small drop remained on my fingers as I poured for the *hunten*.

I saw him sniff, and willed my hand steady as I filled his cup. Up close, his skin had a powdery quality, and flakes were peeling from his temple. I stepped away as the *hunten,* frowning, looked surprised to see his full cup.

Lavinia raised her glass, smiling, though she

142

looked wary.

The room appeared to be waiting, and as he raised his glass someone called a toast to "Lord Carys and Leofe." The echo bounced off the walls as they drank.

I exhaled and closed my eyes, preparing for the next stage, which would inevitably bring me into contact with the *hunten* again.

"Sir." I was interrupted by an urgent hiss from the server next to me. The *hunten* was signalling for more wine. I gratefully took the full carafe from the man, who eyed me suspiciously.

I filled the *hunten's* glass, which he watched, his lips moving soundlessly. Then I felt a drawing sensation as air passed across my body, as though a sheet pulled from atop me. The *hunten's* brow beaded with sweat, but his eyes suddenly focussed on me, jaw taut.

"Why does an emissary of Leocadia hide himself from me?" His voice was like gravel, and his vision drifted away from me and back, as though the effort was difficult to maintain. A flake of skin fell from his temple, and I pulled away.

I had never been touched by a *hunten* before. His grip on my wrist bit like ice, and I dropped the wine as Lavinia lunged hurriedly for his hand.

It happened in an instant, though in hindsight, I saw it clearly. She knocked her own glass as she reached and it cracked against the table, broken shards diving into his skin, spilling blood on the white napkin beneath.

He immediately stood, pushing her away from him, eyes wide and lips pulled back in a grimace.

He raised his bleeding hand as though to strike, and I intervened without thought, grabbing the napkin and taking his hand firmly to stem the blood. His breath quickened as he saw me plainly again.

"Leocadia's reasons are his own."

The *hunten's* grey eyes narrowed but already his hold on the *summonata* that revealed me was slipping, helped perhaps by Magisend's tincture. He stared intently at the napkin pressed to his hand, then back at me.

"Witya," he hissed, and as his nostrils flared the napkin combusted into flames.

Before it hit the ground, I was slammed into it, the *hunten* stood above me, fingers curling into deliberate fists as the invisible forces around me tightened at my throat, forcing air from me. Would I die after all this?

And then a gentler force, releasing the binds, unfurling the iron fingers around my neck and willing air back through my lungs. Magisend must have come. I lifted my head and saw a blurred figure step out of the shadows and fling a silver dagger with a stone hilt. It sliced the air and was drawn as though by design directly into the *hunten's* left eye. His scream was piercing and Lavinia's hands were suddenly at my collar.

"Run, Thomas, you must go," she urged.

144

I scrambled up, searching not only for the hat, which was no longer in my pocket, but the only person who could have thrown that knife.

A rush of force at my back convinced me to abandon the search, and despite the *hunten* calling for men to seize me, most of the guests were staring aghast at the knife protruding from his eye. I ran, ramming into a servant's entry at the side of the room and bursting into the blinding sunlight. I bounced off a horse before launching into a carriage. The footman, talking to a man on the ground, did not notice.

Sitting in the empty carriage, the curtain shielding me from the street, I gasped for breath.

The hat. The blood. Both lost.

Suddenly the carriage dipped and the curtain was flung open by a broad arm.

"Go at once," Gideon commanded the driver as he pulled the curtain closed. He removed the grey hat, placing it on my knee as he sunk down next to me, the carriage lurching forward.

"That was too close a shave."

"The knife," I lamented and Gideon hummed his agreement.

"Still," he pulled a handkerchief from his pocket and unfolded it. Inside, marked with blood around the edges was a shard of broken glass.

"Lavinia?"

"Disappeared. Where to with this?"

I gave directions to Gideon who donned the hat again and called them to the driver, putting his head out once more.

I took the shard and the handkerchief as we approached Magisend's house. Gideon was to go on with the carriage in case its absence was noticed.

The front door opened with a creak, though I had barely stepped onto the doorstep. Magisend was waiting at the window in a deep red dress, a black shawl over her shoulders. She looked as though she were readying to go out.

"What happened? I felt…"

I held out the handkerchief with the shard and Magisend's face flushed.

"Come," she said curtly, gliding quickly across the room and back to the stone workshop.

I followed her into the room which was dark and warm. Magisend removed her shawl and selected a round black stone from the sill by the one window. She dragged her thumbnail in a line down the centre, eyes closed and brow quivering, and then repeated the movement in the opposite direction.

"The blood," she held her hand out, eyes opening on mine.

"The talisman first."

If she was irritated she didn't show it. She simply reached into her pocket and removed a length of black twine. Suspended at the end was a flat amber oval, just larger than a coin. I took it from her, and the stone glowed warm against my palm. My fingertips rested easily in indentations on the reverse as I gazed at the gold twig in the centre. Tiny pockets of air surrounded it, leaves of light.

"It's beautiful - but how can I be sure it works?"

"You can't. Not until it does. It will only work for a suspended being such as yourself. It requires a deeper kind of *summonata* to counteract the force keeping you as you are. It requires love."

I handed over the handkerchief.

"Will it make me visible to the *hunten*?"

"Undoubtedly. They are drawn to *summonata*."

Magisend pushed the shard and kerchief into the air with a flick of her fingers.

Suspended, they orbited each other as Magisend closed her eyes once more and slowly, slowly, flecks of scarlet streamed like sand from each object and formed a quivering sphere of blood.

Magisend drew her other hand up, and the stone which she had marked split down the centre with a crack. I glimpsed a perfect recess for the blood ball and watched entranced as the two halves closed over the blood in mid-air. There was a crack of thunder over the house, and the stone sped downwards until caught in Magisend's palm.

She looked at me, breathing deeply, before turning away and placing the stone in a small wooden box. The stone was marked with a jagged white 'M'.

Before I could ask about its purpose, the door

was thrown wide with a bang and I turned, expecting the *hunten*.

"Magisend, we must leave -" She stopped as though she'd walked into a wall, honey-coloured eyes finding the floor behind my feet.

"Thomas. You're OK."

I looked from Lavinia to Magisend, who exhaled in relief and rushed to pull Lavinia to her.

"I felt-,"

"-it's fine."

They looked at me, Lavinia's eyes anxious and Magisend's hard.

"It was necessary that you felt motivated to obtain the blood," she said simply.

There was a wave in my ears and both women stepped back in unison.

"So, you found a lord's daughter to do your bidding and ensnared her with *wityacraft*?"

Beyond the anger, I remembered Gideon's remonstration that we were pawns to the *witya*. The wrathful injustice louder than the deep, deep ache of the love that I had felt for Lavinia receding between heartbeats.

"I am a *witya*." Lavinia stepped forward slowly and touched my arm. I pulled it back

"No. The shop - the door stuck."

"I played my part well. Until today." She looked at Magisend. "He was dying - I had to free his air from the *hunten* – I fear I was discovered."

Lavinia had used the *summonata*, not

Magisend. The shards from the broken glass had pulled unnaturally into the *hunten's* hand.

"So, you would have let me go with you to New Holland, and wake one day to find you gone?"

There was silence while they glanced at each other.

"You couldn't understand. With this bloodstone - the *hunten* will be---,"

"---no different to you."

I made it to the street before Lavinia caught my arm.

"Thomas… I wasn't going to…I still want to leave with you. I do…love you."

But I could see in her eyes, darting over my face, that she was pleading with herself too to believe the falsehood. My heart was closed.

"Of course, Lavinia, you need to leave now to escape the *hunten*. Or is it Leofe?"

I left her there, a child descending into tears.

As I stalked back to the shop, my fury at the way I had been puppeted and manipulated grated and broiled and churned like rocks in a mill, until people on the street were turning their eyes away, or stepping out of my path.

A cheer came from the next corner, a rallying call from a man holding a banner with a crossed flower. A *witya* catcher.

"A bewitya'd silver dagger, drove like an arrow into Lord Camrys' eye! At his own betrothal!"

His three, armed men watched me approach.

"I know where the *witya* is."

A brass coin was pressed into my hand as the troupe charged back the way I had come.

I looked at the cheap boon. Revulsion at what I'd done, fighting with anger at what had been done to me.

It would be an inconvenience. Magisend would have to leave town; start again in another place. Disguise herself.

A *witya* never succumbed to *witya* catchers.

It was always the innocent that burned.

When Gideon returned to the shop with news that *witya* catchers were planning a burning for Magisend the next day, I'd related what I'd done and why. I'd expected anger, wanted it even. Instead, he'd set tea to brew and placed the hat back on the hook behind the door before voicing what I'd already realised.

"The *hunten* knows your face and Magisend knows everything. You just gave her cause for revenge."

He poured the tea from the leaves of the immortal plant. I was going to miss it.

"I have a ticket to New Holland tomorrow."

We drank in silence a while, before he cleared his throat.

"Such that it matters, there was no news of

Lavinia."

He'd left to find out what he could about the burning the next day. It always happened in the square. I would make my way to the docks while the city was distracted. I finished packing the few things I would need. It was difficult to decide what I would take for myself, and what would remain with Gideon. The dagger was gone, and though the hat would be useful I wanted no more of it. Instead, I took the amulet from Magisend (there was a chance that it might work after all), and the salve that made people agreeable. Gideon had talent enough for that without the salve.

I picked up my rucksack just as the door glided open, and Gideon entered, agitated. Without greeting, he darted around the room, sweeping through drawers and standing back to peer onto high shelves.

"What is it?"

He threw a look at me, startled but didn't stop his search.

"It's not a burning; it's a beheading."

"What?"

"At the docks."

"Why?"

He paused and glanced back at me again.

"The *witya* catchers...were working for Camrys. I'm told he interrogated her...thoroughly."

151

I swallowed.

"What are you looking for?"

"Ismay's ring."

I put my pack down.

The ring was the most magically powerful thing we owned, imbued with a good portion of Ismay's remaining power before she died. We were tasked with safekeeping, until the right time. When used by a *witya* it amplified their hold on the *summonata* - as though two minds were working as one.

It seemed Gideon thought the right time was now, and given I was responsible for Magisend's predicament I didn't disagree.

I dashed upstairs to take the ring from the stone chest in the cupboard by the washroom.

Gideon took the ring with relief.

"What's the plan?"

"It's suspicious that it's at the docks. He may know you'll be there today. You must be careful about how you board. I will do what I can to get to Magisend."

As we ran to the docks, we heard the cheering of the crowd.

"Gideon." I grabbed his forearm, jerking him back. "I'll go this way."

Something in his set face softened for an instant.

"Goodbye, brother."

He said nothing. Just lowered his head after a moment and gripped my forearm back.

Then he was gone, wending his way through the crowd which was gathered before the wooden dais normally used for auctions. Magisend stood atop it, arms behind her back, red dress torn and dirtied. Camrys sat to the side in a stiff chair, watching her carefully.

I wondered dimly how he would get her body, to eat her heart after the spectacle was done.

The largest boat was being loaded, and gilt letters on the side marked her as the vessel that would carry me to safety. I looked back at a roar of delight from the crowd - Gideon was on stage and had cut a lock of Magisend's hair - holding it aloft as though a trophy. As the executioner moved towards him, I saw quick hands at work and Magisend stiffen.

It was best if I was out of sight before anything happened. Turning to the gangway I caught sight of a lone figure standing on the main deck, watching the crowd below.

She looked at me and raised her white-gloved hand in greeting.

Despite my anger with her, I was relieved to see Lavinia safe. The Weavers had built a reputation amongst *wityas*. In time I would forgive. Lavinia would be a customer in New Holland, not a lover.

Another eruption of noise from the crowd, this time shock. I looked for Magisend, but she was gone. The *hunten* stood, growing taller than I'd seen him up close. He screeched his fury, a sound that ricocheted off heads that bowed for cover, as a wave of dust and grit crested over the crowd. Dark clouds broiled overhead and the *hunten* raised his hands, gashes tearing the skin of his face. I turned back to Lavinia whose arms were raised as she stared at the *hunten*.

An instant later, the ship bound for New Holland burst into flames. I stood on the dock and watched the flames devour the ship, before the black smoke billowing from it was too thick to sustain life.

All was silent in the chaos. The heat of the flames pulled my skin tight, and the crowd shoved and stumbled in desperation to avoid the smoke. Gideon slammed into me and sound rushed back, enough for me to heed his shout to run.

It was a long time before Gideon and I spoke. Soot covered our clothes, leaving tracks on our faces where we'd wiped our brows or our chins. There were things I should do, but still I sat there, drinking the tea that Gideon poured.

"She escaped?"

Gideon was silent for a while.

"Magisend passed a message… I can't be sure."

I knew what he meant. *witya* could speak in your mind, but always there was doubt.

"She told Camrys you were Leofe's love, that the two of you boarded a ship yesterday for Barbados." He looked at the ceiling as he spoke.

Suddenly the candles flickered and a fierce

wind howled through the space between
windowpanes.

We rose to our feet.

Magisend was clad all in black. Even her face
was delicately patterned in black ink. She did not
smile.

"She was my daughter."

I felt a chasm of despair as she spoke the words
but it was not my own.

"I am sorry." I swallowed my shame and looked
at her.

She looked at Gideon then.

"I return your gift and leave you another.
Though it weakened me immeasurably, I took her
essence from the ashes while the *hunten* gathered
them for consumption."

I noticed then that despite the candlelight, there
were only two shadows on the wall.

Magisend placed Ismay's ring and a honey-
coloured crystal on the counter of the curiosities shop.

"He believes you are Leocadia," she told me,
and as she looked at me, I realised I was looking
through her... reality was solid and permeating her
form, like she was made of the sheer curtain fabric at
the *hunten's* dining room.

"Who is Leocadia?"

"He has not been seen for centuries. Camrys
fears you."

"But you told him I was gone."

"He knew you were with Leofe. He may think

you are dead."

"I should thank you."

"Should you?"

She grew fainter still before us.

"Protect and guard her memory in secret. Use it as you have done for me."

"The stone - the bloodstone?" I said suddenly, reaching for Magisend as she faded further into shadows. "Where is it?"

"With her. Beyond anyone's reach but hers." She pointed a wispy finger to the crystal.

As the candles flickered, we were alone again.

The Sun and the Rain and The Appleseed

Former intergalactic ambassador Dav watches as his people's last battleship burns signalling the end of war. Now he is left wondering what it means to be a conquered world. Fortunately, his old friend Isaa is there to answer some questions.

About the author: Ada Maria Soto
Ada Maria Soto is a Mexican-American New Zealander with ADHD and dyslexia whose life is chaotically divided between being an author, a publisher, and a parent. Sometimes she even finds time to watch rugby and cricket like a proper Kiwi.

Dav watched from the secluded viewing platform of the orbital wharf as the flames devoured the ship. It was such a waste. He had agreed to the dismantling of the fleet, but his people were in desperate need of materials to rebuild their cities, or even make temporary shelters. But humans did love their symbolism. He couldn't really blame them for that.

Both layers of his eyelids slammed shut at the blinding explosion of the engines; the controlled blaze set within the ship having reached them. A moment later the last of his species' battleships exploded beyond recognition, the debris knocked from any orbit and tumbled into the atmosphere of

157

Pelafix. Different parts of the once great ship flared different colours as it burned.

Isaa placed a hand gently on his shoulder. "There's no way you could have talked them out of it."

"I know." He had wondered if his friend would be with the Earth fleet, or if he was even still alive. Isaa had been 'middle-aged' when they met and liked to call himself old when the war started. It was the risk of friendship with a member of a short-lived species.

Isaa *had* come, drafted onto one of the medical ships, despite his years, to tend to the wounded, advanced braces on his legs to support his ageing bones.

Dav wished he could cry. It wasn't something his species did or could do, but it looked cathartic every time he witnessed a human engage in the act.

Isaa tugged lightly at his shoulder. "Come on, let's get out of here." Dav didn't move. "Take me planet side."

"What?" Dav wasn't sure if he had heard Isaa correctly. His mind no longer seemed to live in the present.

"I played tour guide on Earth for almost thirty years, and you said if I ever got to Pelafix you would show me around. Here I am and I'm not getting any younger."

"I-" Dav knew Isaa was trying to distract him from his grief, but the idea was ludicrous. "There are guards everywhere and the cities are rubble."

"So? You've been reinstated as a planetary ambassador, and my drafted ass is a major. I think between the two of us we can make it happen."

A small part of him did like the idea of seeing his world through the eyes of his friend, but it was so fundamentally changed, even before the human fleet had arrived.

"Remember when I took you to the Yellowstone Volcano Fields and you said you would show me the Tallren—"

"Tellaress," he corrected.

"A whole field of multicoloured mud pools. So, let's get onto a shuttle for 'official diplomatic business' and look at mud."

Dav saw the skin of his own hands flush a light blue of amusement for the first time in possibly years. "Yes, Tellaress, a diplomatic necessity."

Isaa was mostly correct, and getting onto a shuttle was as easy as showing their credentials. A surface vehicle proved more difficult, as the majority of those still functioning had been commandeered by the military.

Dav stood back as Isaa informed a young soldier that he was a doctor and needed the ambassador to show him something, with the unspoken implication that there was some sort of possible medical emergency. There were many medical emergencies still, but a human doctor would be of little good to his people. Humans were nightmarishly durable compared to his species. This left their medicine a combination of modulated poisons and detailed violence that would kill anyone else. But this wasn't common knowledge. In the end, it was still enough of a carefully spun half-truth that they were soon headed out of the city.

He kept his eyes mostly on his feet as Isaa drove, only glancing up occasionally to show his credentials at checkpoints. Years before his leaders had so brutally underestimated human tenacity, he had thought of showing Issa his world. They passed a pile of rubble that had been a famous sculpture garden. It would have been a highlight. The musical archives next to it were still half standing. That was something.

Even as they left the city limits there were great gouges in the land where pieces of their once mighty fleet had been driven to the ground by the 'primitive' ships of Earth.

Isaa reached across the car and put a hand on his shoulder again. "I think we're past the worst of it."

"What?"

"You're maroon."

Dav caught a glimpse of the shifting colour of his hands. You'd think he was a child these days with no control, every feeling painted in colour across his skin. "I fear I will always be trapped in the worst of this."

"Human medicine actually has a term for that."

"Of course, you do. You're warriors."

"Nah. We're petty, stubborn, clever monkeys who don't know when to quit. Big difference."

"That's what I tried to explain to the grand council before … before."

Isaa squeezed his shoulder in a distant echo of a hug and let silence fill the vehicle once more. Eventually the ground became rough, not from the falling of ships but from long-ago movement of the land itself.

"We will have to walk from here. It's not far." He would have worried over Isaa's advanced age, but the braces that let him stand through hours of surgery also let him take long, easy strides over rock and rubble. "We came here often when I was young." He was glad to see the information signs for visitors were untouched, as was a bench that allowed someone to sit and observe the pools as well as the crumbled temples beyond.

Isaa sat on the bench next to him and leaned back. "Okay, I'm impressed. I would not have thought it was possible to get that many different shades of … mud in one place."

Dav gestured across the vast field of pools as his teachers did when he was young. "The old religion believed that this is where life started on the planet, and the pools mimic every possible colour of

161

our skin. Pilgrims would come to the temples in their thousands. Then new gods took over, and then science told us the old religion might have been right all along and the first life could have occurred on the edges of these pools."

The wind shifted and, for a moment, whirlpools rippled the surface of the primordial ponds. Isaa reached into one of the large pockets of his coat and pulled out a small box. "Sorry I couldn't get anything fresh, but this should have you hearing colours and tasting music. Snagged it from a post-op lunch cart."

There was a picture of a shiny red apple on the box and a straw attached to the side. "Thank you." He opened the box and took a sip, letting the soothing tingle wash down his throat, followed by a pleasant numbness. If he paced himself, he could drink most of the juice box before the proper hallucinations kicked in. "The old pilgrims were said to receive visions from the gods. It was probably a build-up of fumes from the pools."

"Back in the day, we had oracles who did the same. They were said to have the gift of prophecy. They'd give visions of the future to the good and the great of the ancient world. Or really whoever showed up." Isaa took a small bottle of pale brown liquid from his pocket.

Dav caught the smell of fermentation when it was opened. He took another sip of his own drink. "How close did we get to Earth? I know what we were told, but I could tell they were lies. Io is taken,

Mars is taken, Luna is taken. But then there was quiet. You can't take the moon and not have Earth in the next day, but weeks and weeks went by…" He tried to lick his lips as they began to go numb.

"Proxima Centauri." Isaa's voice was flat as he cut in.

Dav was sure he must be turning suddenly green with humour. "Proxima Centauri." He rolled the human name of Mestrisin Nine around his mouth.

"We knew once the Proxima Colonies had been taken, the next stop was Earth. The fleet pulled back, mined every slipstream entrance point, and armed everything in the solar system that could be pressurised. Cargo ships, luxury yachts. They even reprogramed the asteroid mining drones to throw rocks." Isaa tipped back most of his bottle. "Your ships dropped into a minefield in the Neptune orbit, and the ones that survived that tried again at the Saturn gate. You probably lost half your fleet in twelve hours. And after that…" Isaa shrugged.

"You drove us back across the galaxy right into our own gravity well." The colours of the pools were beginning to sing to him, and he could taste the rustling of the breeze through tall grass. He decided he needed prophecy more than he needed to pace himself, and emptied the box of juice meant for children and the ill.

"What is going to happen to us?" he asked, the question meant for Isaa as much as it was meant for the ghosts of long-dead gods that might still be listening. "I know what is in the peace treaty, I helped write it, but what is really going to happen?"

"Do you want me to guess based on history?"

"Yes."

Isaa sighed and stared out over the pools himself. "We'll take over all government and administrative positions for a few years, to help out, of course. Once we let you have elections again, we'll rig the first few, just to make sure. Can't have anyone with militaristic or populous leanings running the place."

His words were beginning to spell themselves in dancing steam in front of Dav's eyes.

"We'll send teachers to help out with the orphaned and displaced children. So of course, they'll learn human languages, and any history of the last few years will be taught to them from the human perspective."

Dav nodded. It all made sense. What better way to take revenge upon a vanquished enemy than to remake their children in your image?

"You're going to meet Jesus, I can guarantee that. Not sure which version. Depends who gets a ship together first. Probably the Catholics or the Baptists, but I wouldn't rule out the Mormons. They might see this as a chance for a giant door knock."

Across the coloured thermal pools were tall shimmering forms where the grand temples of his ancestors once stood. Maybe the old gods were listening to the prophecy as well.

164

"Do you think someone will plant apple trees?"

"Apples are an intoxicant, narcotic, and hallucinogenic to your species. There will be apple trees as far as the eye can see."

Dav felt drops of water roll down his face and, for a moment, he thought he had achieved the impossible and was finally crying. "It never used to rain this hard," he said instead.

Isaa unfolded a small umbrella and moved in close, trying to shield him from the weather, but it did little to keep them dry. "It's probably extra particulates in the atmosphere. They'll settle out eventually."

"And then someone can start planting the apple seeds."

My Best Friend

What starts out as an innocent bit of insurance fraud goes awry because of a woman.

About the author: Tim Owen

Tim Owen is the founder and leader of Auckland's Northshore Writers Group. He has published many articles as a feature travel writer in South Africa, three novels and a few self-help books. He is currently working on a sci-fi mystery adventure.

Tom and I walked across the hot, sparkling sand of the deserted beach to the *Firefly*. The sun glistened off his muscular shoulders and I felt my usual pang of envy.

The sailboat swayed and bobbed gently at the edge of the water as the waves lapped at the hull, inviting it to play. The boat needed some tender loving care; the mast was cracked and peering over the starboard side and the deck was a wobble of loose planks.

No TLC today, though.

"Fifty percent, yeah?" Tom said. He was my oldest friend, my bestie, my bud. He was also a numbers guy, an insurance broker by trade, which was a bonus.

"Fifty, fifty," I agreed.

We shook on it, a gentleman's agreement; there would be no paper trail for this part of the deal and no need for one; we trusted each other with our lives.

167

"Well, sign here and your 81-footer luxury yacht will be fully insured against fire and theft," he said.

I signed the electronic insurance application using the stylus Tom proffered and turned towards the little boat I had recently purchased on Trademe for $1000.

"You sure we'll get away with this?" I asked. It seemed too easy.

"Don't worry, everything's taken care of. I filed a fake invoice from a contact in Dubai, had to pay him a small fee, of course, but that'll come out of my share. I'm not greedy."

"Do we need to wait, or…?"

Tom laughed. "It's all electronic, Nate Mate, done and dusted. The contract is active. Shall we start the fireworks?"

"Just a sec."

I took a can of blood red spray paint out of my rucksack and sprayed over the wavy blue letters spelling *Firefly* on the side of this little wreck.

Tom raised an eyebrow.

"*Maggie?*" he said. "That seems a little harsh, considering what we're about to do. Trouble in paradise?"

"Nope," I replied. "No trouble. I just think Maggie would be tickled to have a ship named after her, don't you?"

"Except, this isn't a ship," he reminded me.

"That's not what your little electronic gizmo says, it says it's a grand yacht worthy of princes and porn stars."

168

"Touche."

We pushed the *Maggie* out, wading until we were neck-deep before clambering aboard. I had left two jerry cans of petrol on the deck beside the rusty anchor, which was not attached to a chain and throwing it overboard would have been tantamount to littering.

We treaded lightly as we stepped around the warped deck, tipping the contents of the jerry cans onto the untreated, dry timber. "So, what's the current value of my new Ferretti yacht?" I asked.

"Replacement value? About three mill. More, if you wait a year."

"That's okay, I'll settle for the three million. I'm not greedy either."

Tom laughed. "Good call, Nate! Wouldn't want to waste all this perfectly good petrol, would we?"

Tom tossed his empty jerry can into the tiny cabin, and I followed suit. With the delicious, intoxicating fumes of petrol infusing the air, he said, "All set?"

"One last thing." I turned to retrieve the anchor which was hulking on the deck behind me like a big, rusted fishing hook.

"What are you going to do with that?"

I hefted it up by the shaft and plunged it point first into my friend's belly.

"*Oh!*" he said. He seemed surprised, and his eyes registered confusion.

The force of the blow pushed him backwards, his foot twisting through one of the rotten floorboards with the unmistakable *snap* of a dry twig in a silent

169

forest. He looked a right dick, lying there with his leg sticking up at an awkward angle, and a giant fishhook protruding from his muscled torso. The rust from the anchor seemed to drip ochre and Tom had the most stupid expression on his handsome face.

I stepped over him, minding the dodgy planks and pooling blood and retrieved a Zippo lighter from his pocket. "Gonna need this," I remarked.

"Wait," I said, feigning surprise. "There's an inscription. Can't quite make it out. Looks like *Darling Tom, I burn for you, always. Maggie.*"

His eyes widened as comprehension settled in behind them.

"*Awww,*" I said with a mocking tilt to my head. "That's so *sweet.*"

I flicked the lighter into flame and held it above him.

"Wait!" he blurted, holding his palms up towards me defensively. Blood trickled from the corner of his mouth. "Nate, it's not---"

I dropped the lighter where I stood, leaping overboard into the warm Pacific Ocean. I waded to the sand and made my way to the wharf, where I stood and watched the flames engulf my "ship."

I could hear Tom's screams now, and I wished he would shut up so I could enjoy the moment in peace. The sound of the fire was muted, like a crackling wind in my ears, until it found the little boat's gas cooker's cylinder.

Kaboom!

It was splendid.

Also, no more unpleasant screaming.

I stayed until the boat had disintegrated and the remnants of the fire descended into the water, steam rising like a beautiful mist above the idyllic azure surface. With the sun on my chest and money to burn, I felt exhilarated.

Soon, life would be perfect.

I arrived at the car and with serendipitous timing, my phone rang. I answered.

"Hey, Maggie, we were just talking about you."

I opened the glove compartment to check that the gun was still there and set off home.

The Wharf, the Branch and the Future

The following is an outside entry by Sylvia Apostol. Her writing holds much promise, and we look forward to seeing what she comes up with in the future.

About the author: Sylvia Apostol

It was just before my 13th birthday when I wrote *The Wharf, the Branch, and the Future*. At that time, I was starting college. Now, two years on, my wharf is filled with so many different ships. As for my future... I guess I still have to wait.

This story can be anything you interpret it to be. It could be a person, a memory, or a story to help you through your grief, because everyone has a hard time sometimes and what you need is someone who understands. All you have to do is think to a deeper level and forget about understanding. There is no right or wrong interpretation, once you read it, it's yours...

There is nothing worse than watching a person you promised you would never forget, forget you.

It's like standing on a wharf watching the flames devouring the relationship. The precious cargo of that ship, the happiest, most loving memories, now going up in smoke.

The branch connecting us had split in two, or maybe, we were leaves and one of us had been blown away, whatever it was, it felt like a giant hand squeezing my body to the point of suffocation.

I know every story has an ending, but this one had ended so… abruptly. It surprised me that a person could forget me and our story so quickly. I could not comprehend it. A ship so sturdy was being destroyed right in front of my eyes, reduced to a pile of soggy ashes. It was as if we did not even exist anymore. Maybe our bodies were still on that ship, and we were burning too, or a wall had been built separating us. But, to my knowledge, we had disappeared. Had I really been forgotten in the span of, what, a month?

What could I have done to go back and prevent that ship from igniting? Nothing, because that was in the past. The one thing I could never do was go back. The only time we had was the present and that was gone.

Anger. All those years, now knowing they were wasted time I can never get back. I felt a concoction of feelings but anger, it was so strong, a feeling of inner frustration, unimportance, and irritation. Questions clouded my wretched mind, questions underscored with rage. Maybe I could have saved it. But I didn't, I stood on the wharf and watched the love between us incinerate. Why? I did not know, I had the power to stop it at that moment. The annoyance and hatred I felt for myself… Why hadn't I *done* anything? All I wanted was to go back, back to the old memories, moments, laughter. Back to when my wharf was full of all different types of ships.

I longed to experience those times again, now knowing that they wouldn't last, I wanted to experience them better, appreciate them more.

My heart was shattering like glass, I had thought that if you listened closely, you could hear the glass crunching after each heartbeat. No matter how much I tried to swallow the lump in my throat, it kept coming back. No matter how much I tried to stop the tears from rolling, they kept flowing. There was nothing left of my happiness, it was utterly depleted.

How could I stop this crippling feeling of sadness and depression from eating me whole? What could I possibly do to stop this painful affliction? I did not know… so I thought. I let my mind wander through hallways it had never been to before. I let it revisit old ships, old branches. I looked through the old memories, and the tears started overflowing again.

I thought. Then I realised, every story had to end. But new people and more ships might fill my wharf. New relationships and more leaves on my branch. The future had not ended yet, no, it had only just begun. Who knows what my wharf might hold?

No one.

More from
THE NORTHSHORE WRITERS

With their latest collection of thrilling short stories, The North Shore Writers Group takes you on a journey that spans a multitude of genres. Readers will find romance with unintended consequences, corruption, menacing cows, portals to alternate universes, trapped and tortured souls and secrets that haunt the shadows.

From the eerie to the absurd, reality is challenged, nothing is as it seems, nor will it ever look quite the same again.

www.ingramcontent.com/pod-product-compliance
Lightning Source LLC
Chambersburg PA
CBHW061233170626
46809CB00007B/2661